Mates, Dates &
Sleepover Secrets.

C. Hopkins

Cathy Hopkins lives in North London with her handsome husband and three cats. She spends most of her time locked in a shed at the bottom of the garden pretending to write books, but is actually in there listening to music, hippie dancing and talking to her friends on e-mail.

Occasionally, she is joined by Molly, the cat who thinks she is a copy-editor and likes to walk all over the keyboard rewriting and deleting any words she doesn't like.

The other cats have other jobs.

Barny likes to lie on his back in the grass, stare at the clouds and create poetry. (Sadly, none of it has been published, as it has been hard to find someone to translate it from Catspeak, but he and Cathy are ever hopeful.)

Maisie, the third cat, was worried that Cathy may have forgotten what it is like to be a teenager, so she does her best to remind her. She does it very well. She ignores everybody and only comes in to eat, sleep and occasionally wearily say 'miwhhf' (this means 'whatever' in Catspeak).

Apart from that, Cathy has joined the gym and spends more time than is good for her making up excuses as to why she hasn't got time to go.

Mates, Dates and Sleepover Secrets

Cathy Hopkins

PICCADILLY PRESS • LONDON

Big thanks to Brenda, Jude, Margot and the team at Piccadilly. And Rosemary Bromley at Juvenilia. Big ta to Steve Lovering for all his support and getting to know TJ as well as I did. And to Phil (The Path) Howard Jones for his bizarre emails which inspired the voice of Hannah. To Steve Denham for his input on magazine layouts. To Richard (Not So Scary Dad) Jeffrey. To Stephen Jeffrey for traipsing round Battersea Dogs' Home with me. And last but not least, thanks to the A team: Jenni Hertzburg, Becca Crewe, Rachel Hopkins and Grace O'Malley. And seeing as I've turned into Gwyneth Paltrow when she got her Oscar I'd better mention my mum and dad, family, friends, the postman, the milkman, my cats and God. (Did I leave anybody out?)

First published in Great Britain in 2002
by Piccadilly Press Ltd.,
5 Castle Road, London NW1 8PR

A catalogue record for this book is available from the British Library

ISBN: 1 85340 795 X (trade paperback)

13 15 17 19 20 18 16 14 12

Printed and bound in Great Britain by Bookmarque Ltd.

Typeset by Textype Typesetters, Cambridge
Design by Judith Robertson
Cover design by Steve Lovering

Set in 11.5pt Bembo and Tempus

Chapter 1

Noola the Alien Girl

'We are the champions, *we are the champions*,' sang some Stupid Boy outside the window of the girls' changing-room.

'How sad is that?' asked Melanie Jones as she rubbed strawberry-scented body lotion on to her legs. 'We beat them three weeks running and they win *once* and think they're it.'

'Yeah,' I said as I pulled my hair back and plaited it. 'Today,' I said, raising my voice so that Stupid Boy could hear outside, 'was a mere blip in our team's otherwise excellent performance.'

'Yay,' chorused the rest of our team who were in various states of undress after the football match.

'You woz rubbish,' shouted Stupid Boy.

I shoved my stuff into my sports bag and stepped

outside into the dazzling June sunshine. There was Stupid Boy – namely Will Evans, goalie from the boys' team.

'You talking to me?' I asked.

Will tried to square up to me, which was difficult seeing as I'm five foot seven and he's a squirt at five foot four.

'Yeah,' he said to my nose.

'In that case, would you mind using the correct grammar? It's you *were* rubbish, not you *woz*.'

Will went red as the group of lads around him sniggered.

He stuck his tongue out at me.

'Oh,' I yawned. 'Like I'm *really* scared now.'

By now, most of the girls' team had finished changing and had come out to see what was happening. It was always the same. Every Saturday, after the match, the games continued off the pitch. Often with the girls bombing the boys with balloons swollen with water from the changing-room taps.

I picked up my bag to go home. I'd got bored with it all in the last few weeks. I was sure there had to be a better way to get a boy's attention than splattering him with water.

Anyway, it was Saturday and that meant lunch with Mum and Dad. Dad insists that we eat together as 'a family' on the rare occasions that he's not working. What family? I think. It's not like I have hundreds of brothers and sisters. Only Marie who's twenty-six and left home to live in Southampton years ago and Paul who's twenty-one and been away studying in Bristol.

'Oi, Watts,' called Will.

'The name's TJ, actually,' I said, turning back.

'TJ? What kind of name is that?' sniggered Mark, one of the other boys on the team. 'TJ. *TJ.*'

I tried to think of something clever to say. 'It's *my* kind of name,' I said, for want of anything better.

I didn't want to get into the real reason. I'd never hear the end of it. My full name is Theresa Joanne Watts. Like, yeah. How dull and girlie is that? But Paul has called me TJ since I was a baby and it stuck. Much better than Theresa Joanne. But I wasn't going to explain all this to the nerdie boys from St Joseph's High. If they knew I hated my real name, then that's what I'd be called for ever.

'OK then, *TJ.* You and me,' said Will, pointing at a picnic table by the football pitch. 'Over there. Arm-wrestling.'

Now this was tempting. Arm-wrestling was my major talent.

I took a quick look at my watch. I had time.

'OK, Evans. Prepare to die.'

We took up our positions opposite each other at the table and both put our arms out, elbows down. A small crowd soon gathered round as we grasped hands.

'Ready,' said Mark, 'steady, GO.'

I strained to keep my lower arm upright as we began to arm-wrestle.

'Come *on*, TJ,' cried the girls.

'Come *on*, Will,' cried the boys.

'Hey, TJ, there's a guy looking for you outside the boys' changing-room,' said Dave, the boys' team captain as he came out to join us.

'Nice try,' I said, not looking up. I wasn't going to break my concentration for the oldest trick in the book. Plus, Dave was A Bit Of A Hunk and I usually said or did something stupid when one of his super species was around. I made myself focus. The crowd around was beginning to get excited as I kept my arm firm and Will's started to weaken.

'Show him, TJ,' said one of the girls.

I could feel my strength wavering as Will fought back and my arm wobbled. Then I summoned every ounce of energy and *slam*, Will's arm was on the table.

'Hurrah,' cheered the girls, then began singing. '*We* are the champions. *We* are the champions. Champions, the champions, champions of Europe.'

'*Stupid* girls,' said Will, rubbing his hand and going to unlock his bike. 'Anyway, we won the footie and that's what really counts. So there.'

'Oh, grow up,' I called, as I walked away.

'There really is someone looking for you, TJ,' said Dave, catching up with me and putting his hand on my shoulder.

As I turned and looked into his denim-blue eyes, my stomach went all fluttery.

'I didn't say it to distract you. Over there, see?' he

8

continued. 'Hippie guy with dark hair and an earring.'

I looked to where he pointed and there was my brother Paul, a short distance away.

'*Nihingyah*,' I said to Dave, who looked at me quizzically.

I shrugged and turned back towards my brother, who gave me a wave. No point in explaining, I thought, as I made my way over to Paul. Dave would never understand how I get taken over by Noola the Alien Girl when confronted by Boy Babes. She doesn't know many words. Mainly ones like *uhyuh*, *yunewee* and *nihingyah*, which I think means, 'oh, yeah' and 'thanks', in alien-speak.

'Hey, TJ,' said Paul, giving me a hug.

'Hey,' I said and hugged him back.

'Bit old for you, isn't he?' taunted Will, as he rode past on his bike.

'Get a life, you perv,' I said, as I linked with Paul and drew him away from the crowds. 'He's my *brother*.'

Paul grinned and looked back at Will. 'Looks like I'm interrupting something.'

'As if.'

'Come on, you can tell me. Someone special?'

'Only the local pond-life,' I said. 'You home for lunch?'

'Yeah,' sighed Paul and ran his fingers through his hair. 'Bad vibes. Thought I'd escape awhile and come and find you.'

'Scary Dad still mad with you?'

Paul nodded. 'And some. The way he goes on, anyone

would think I'd committed a murder rather than dropped out of university. But you know how he is.'

Boy, did I know! Night and day, me and Mum had to listen to him going on . . . and on . . . Paul has ruined his life. Paul has spoilt the opportunity of a lifetime. Paul has wasted his talent. If only Paul were more like Marie. He was always a dreamer. He had it too easy. What's to become of him? Where did we go wrong?

On and on and *on*.

See, Dad's a bigwig hospital consultant. Mum's a GP. Even my sister, Marie, is a doctor. Plan was, Paul was to join the club, follow in the family footsteps sort of thing. Only he never wanted to. He wanted to be a musician. He went along with the doctor bit. Got good grades. Got into medical school. Did a year. Did a self-awareness type weekend in London. Saw the light or something. Dropped out of college. Grew his hair. Started spouting self-help jargon. Got into alternative medicine and rejected pretty well everything Dad stands for. Oops.

Dad mad.

Mum sad.

Me though, I'm glad. Not that he's having a hard time, of course. I feel sorry for him getting all the stick from Dad, but Dad's got me lined up to be a doctor as well. Ew, no thanks. Way too much blood. I want to be a writer, so I'm hoping all this with Paul will pave the way for my eventual fall from grace.

'Seriously though. Looks like you had a lot of admirers

there,' said Paul, pointing back to the football pitch.

'Nah,' I said. 'Boys are never interested in me.'

'Looked to me like they were *very* interested.'

'Only because I'm the arm-wrestling champ,' I grinned. 'I had to show them what's what after we lost at footie this morning.'

Paul gave me a look and sighed. 'TJ, you're impossible. Wake up and smell the hormones, kiddo. You're easily the prettiest girl on the team.'

'Me, pretty? Yeah, right. Get real.'

'I am,' he said and pulled on my plait.

'You're only saying that because you're my brother.'

'No,' he said. 'You're always doing yourself down. Like you can't see that you're gorgeous.'

'Now I know you're kidding. I couldn't get a boy if I tried.'

'Have you tried?'

I shrugged. 'Er, dunno. Not really. But . . . it's like, I either talk alien or go into my Miss Strop bossy act and start correcting their grammar. I mean. D'oh. How flirty is that? Or else, I terrify them with my super-human strength. You know, humiliate them by winning at arm-wrestling. Very girlie. Not. It just never seems to come out right.'

'It will, TJ,' said Paul gently.

'But *when*? Most girls in my year have sore lips from snogging. Me? The only sore bits I've got are bruises from where some boy has kicked me in a football game. I'm hopeless. Hannah was so good at the boy thing. They used to really like her.'

Paul looked at me with concern. 'Sorry about Hannah. Mum told me. When did she go?'

'Fortnight ago,' I said as my eyes stung with tears. I was still feeling raw about her leaving but I was determined not to cry like a baby in front of Paul. Hannah was my best friend. And she'd just gone to live in South Africa. Yeah, in South Africa. Not exactly the kind of place you can hop on a bus to when you fancy a chat. I was missing her like mad.

'You'll soon find new friends,' said Paul.

Arghhh. If another person says that to me, I think I shall scream. In fact, if Paul wasn't my brother I'd have socked him. People don't understand. *You'll soon find other friends*, like you can go out and buy one in the supermarket.

'I don't *want* new friends,' I said. 'I want Hannah back.'

Hannah was a one-off. A real laugh. I knew I'd never meet anyone like her ever again. It was her that came up with the nickname Scary Dad for my father. And with her around, boys never noticed I was tongue-tied or awkward – she babbled enough for both of us. I could hide behind her and they never realised that my cool was actually frozen shy.

As we turned into our road, we almost ran into Mr Kershaw on the pavement in front of us. He was walking his dog Drule. Or rather, Drule was walking him. Drule is a big black Alsatian and Mr Kershaw was having a hard time holding on to the lead.

'He can't wait to get to the park,' he grinned as Drule yanked him forward.

I laughed and turned to go in our gate but Paul stopped me.

'Actually, TJ, don't go in yet. I didn't just come to walk you home. I've got something to tell you.'

'What?'

As he shifted about on his feet, something told me that I wasn't going to like what he had to say.

Chapter 2

Giggling
Girlies

'Hey, TJ,' called Scott Harris from his bedroom window.
'Hang on, I'm coming down.'

Before I could answer, his head disappeared and the
window closed, so I sat on the front step outside our
house and waited for him. The Harris family has lived
next door to us ever since we moved here when I was
seven, so Scott is the next best thing I have to a brother
besides Paul. Scott's two years older than me and lately
has discovered girls. Or rather, girls have discovered him.
He's cute in that Richie from Five kind of way and there's
often a group of giggling girlies outside his gate. Scott
liked to talk his latest conquests over with me and no
doubt that's what he wanted to do now.

'TJ,' called Mum from inside. 'Lunch'll be on the table
in five minutes.'

'Coming,' I called back. 'Just got to see Scott for a mo.'

I was glad Scott was coming over, as I badly needed

someone to talk to. I was hoping he'd distract me from the sinking feeling in the pit of my stomach. Paul had just told me that he was going travelling with his girlfriend, Saskia. For a year, maybe two. Starting with Goa, then maybe Australia and Tahiti. First Hannah, now Paul. What was going on? My two favourite people disappearing out of my life in less than ten days.

'Where've you been?' said Scott, appearing round the rhododendron bush in our front garden.

I opened my mouth to say 'football', but he was off again before I had time.

'Been looking everywhere for you.'

'Good,' I said. 'Because *I* want to talk to you.'

'Why? What's happening?'

'Oh, everything,' I began. 'You know Paul dropped out and everything, well, now he's off travelling. Hannah's gone. I . . .'

'Really? Cool,' said Scott, looking at his watch.

D'oh? I thought. No. Not cool. 'Scott, are you listening?'

'Yeah. Course. But I need to ask a favour first.'

I sighed. 'What?'

'Hot date,' said Scott, with a grin. 'I need to borrow a fiver. Just for today. I'll give it back to you next week when I get my allowance.'

Yeah, I thought, you said that last week when I lent you two quid. But then I didn't want him to think I was a cheapskate. No one likes a cheapskate. I was sure he'd give it back to me in the end.

I rummaged around in my sports bag, found my purse and pulled out the fiver pocket money that Mum had given me that morning.

'Thanks,' said Scott. 'You're a pal.'

'So who's the sad victim this afternoon?' I asked.

'Jessica Hartley. She's from your school.'

I nodded. I knew Jessica all right. She was hard to miss. Just Scott's type, glam and girlie with long blonde hair.

'Yeah. She's in the year above me. In Year 10. Anyway, as I was saying, Paul's leaving tomorrow, Hannah's gone and it feels like . . .'

'Actually,' interrupted Scott, 'talking about your school. Do you know Nesta Williams?'

'Yes,' I said. 'She's in my class.'

Scott looked as though he'd won the lottery. 'Wow. You're kidding? How *fantastic*. She's like, a five-star babe. Could you put in a word for me?'

For some reason this irked me. Who did he think I was? First the bank that likes to say yes, now a dating agency?

'What about Jessica?' I asked.

'What about Jessica?'

'Well, if she's your girlfriend, would she like you asking about Nesta?'

'Hey. Not my fault,' said Scott with a wide smile. 'So many girls, only one me.'

My jaw dropped open, but then I realised he was

joking. At least, I *think* he was joking. Sometimes, he acted as though he believed he really was God's gift to women.

'Oh, poor you having to share yourself around us miserable impoverished girls,' I said.

Scott laughed. 'You know, you're really cool, TJ. You're so easy to talk to. Like one of the boys.'

'Thanks,' I said, feeling chuffed with the compliment. Easy to talk to? Maybe that was it. I didn't need to worry about being tongue-tied or saying the wrong thing. I don't need to talk, only listen. Maybe there was hope for me after all.

'Anyway – Nesta. What's she like?'

It was out before I could stop myself. 'Oh – a complete airhead.'

I felt a bit rotten saying that, as I don't really know Nesta beyond the fact that she's the prettiest girl in the whole school. I've never spent any time with her.

'Airhead's OK,' grinned Scott. 'It's not like I want her to *talk* to.'

'Yeah, right,' I said, suddenly feeling miffed. Maybe it *wasn't* such a compliment that I was easy to talk to? Oh, I don't know. Boys. They confuse me.

'Wanna arm-wrestle?' I asked.

Scott looked at me as if I was out of my mind. *'What?'*

'Arm . . . oh, nothing,' I said, as I saw Jessica tottering up the road in strappy high heels. 'Your date's here.'

Jessica appeared at the gate and looked surprised to see

me. She looked fantastic in a tiny white tank top and white jeans with diamante bits sewn up the seams.

'Hey,' said Scott, leaping up and going over to her. 'You look good.'

Jessica was staring at me as though I'd just crawled out from under a stone.

'Thanks,' she said and jerked her thumb at me. 'Sister?'

'Next-door neighbour,' said Scott. 'You know each other from school, right?'

I smiled at Jessica, but she didn't smile back. 'Can't say I've noticed her,' she said. Then, flicking her hair as if dismissing me, she turned away.

'See you later,' winked Scott. He put his arm round Jessica, snuggled into her and whispered something in her ear.

Jessica giggled and they disappeared off down the road.

'Er . . . nice to meet you, too,' I called after them.

Huh, I thought. You can act as superior as you like, Jessica Hartley, but I know Scott's got his eye on someone else. One week and you'll be history. So there. Stick that in your diet yoghurt and eat it.

I sat out for a bit longer. So much for my heart-to-heart with Scott. Paul was leaving and I felt miserable. Who could I talk to? Scott was a waste of time.

'TJ,' called Mum's voice. 'Lunch. On the table. *Now.*'

As I got up to go in, I saw Mr Kershaw and Drule go past again. Mr Kershaw was jabbering away to Drule and the dog was looking up at him as if he understood every word.

That's it, I thought. I'm going to ask Mum for a dog. She said I could have a pet ages ago. A best friend of the furry kind. One who won't leave the country.

Why didn't I think of it before?

---

email: Outbox (1)
From: goody2shoes@psnet.co.uk
To: hannahnutter@fastmail.com
Date: 9 June
Subject: Norf London blues

Hi Hannah

Miss you loads.

Idea: why don't we run away to LA? I can write film scripts and you can be a dancer?

Bad news: our team lost at footie. But then, you were our best player so I guess it's to be expected. Don't your parents realise the devastation it has caused nationally by removing you from the country?

My bro Paul is leaving. Off to Goa. With Saskia.

Ag. Agh. *Agherama.* I'm losing all my friends.

Scary Dad is in v bad mood. It's not *my* fault Paul wants to play the bass guitar and be a hippie instead of being a doctor. Atmosphere at home awful.

Good news: Beat that scab Evans at arm-wrestling. Hahahaha.

Mum says I can have a dog. Suggest you get one too if your mum will allow until you settle in at school. Dog – man's best friend etc etc. We're going to go next weekend to look for one.

Paul is staying the night. Hurrah. And for Sunday lunch. After that he's off and I will be All On My Own.

And guess what? Jessica Hartley from Year 10 is going out with Scott. But he fancies Nesta Williams. Hahahaha.

If another person says – you'll soon make new friends, I vill 'ave to keell them.

I am starting a collection of made-up books by made-up authors. For example:

Medical Hosiery by Serge Icklestockings

Modern Giants by Hugh Mungous

Please send contributions.

Tata for now

TJ

PS: Confucius say: man with no front garden look forlorn.

email: Inbox (1)
From: hannahnutter@fastmail.com
To: goody2shoes@psnet.co.uk
Date: 9 June
Subject: Cape cool

Hasta banana baby

Miss you too, megalooney.

   Keep your chinola up. It's hard for me too. Everything's
so differentio here. It's supposed to be winter but it's hot
hot HOT. Cape Town is mega. You must come and visit. So
far been up Table Mountain. Pretty cool. Though hot.
Haha. And to the beach. Pretty hot though cool. Haha.
There are loads of beaches here, everyone hangs out there.
Boys here look more healthy than back home. All suntans
and white teeth. Still stupid though if the one next door is
anything to go by. His name's Mark. He's OK but he asked
me to a barbie at his house and he eats with his mouth open
and you can see all his food. Ew. Gross. He'll never get off
with anyone if he doesn't learn to eat properly.

   Book titles. Hmmm. Let me think.
   OK.
   Pain In the Neck by Lauren Gitis
   Hahahahahaha.

   Chow bambino
   Love you muchomucho
   Hannah

   Confucius say: who say I say all those things they say I
say?
   Arf. Arf.

Chapter 3

The
Wrinklies

'Stand close,' said Mum as she pointed the camera at us in the back garden. 'Put your hand on Paul's shoulder, Richard. And *try* and look as though you like him a bit.'

Dad shuffled about behind us then finally put his hand on Paul's shoulder. 'Might be more appropriate if Paul put *his* hand in *my* pocket,' he muttered.

'Oh, for heaven's sake,' said Mum. 'Enough now. You made your point over lunch. This is our last day together as a family before Paul leaves for Goa. Try and act like a grown-up.'

Paul and I tried not to laugh as Dad looked at the lawn like a naughty schoolboy. Quite an achievement seeing as he's in his sixties, but Mum can be Scary Mum to his Scary Dad when she likes. She gets a look in her eye and you know she's not to be messed with. Hannah used to call my parents the Wrinklies because they're so ancient. Mum had me when she was forty-five and Dad was fifty-three. They thought they'd finished having children with

Paul. Then seven years later, along came yours truly. I think I was what is commonly known in birth terms as A Surprise. Or A Mistake. Whatever. All I know is that I have the oldest parents of anyone in school. I used to get embarrassed when there'd be all these young mums in T-shirts and jeans waiting after school, then along would come my mum or dad in their 'comfy clothes' looking more like my grandparents. I started telling people that Mum and Dad were actually the same age as normal parents but they'd been captured by aliens one summer and kept as an experiment on their spaceship for two days. The trauma made their hair grow white and they grew old before their time. One girl in my class actually believed me.

Mum took her picture and Dad headed for the car.

So much for our last day together as a family before Paul's trip, I thought, as I watched Dad reverse his Mercedes down the driveway and zoom off towards his golf club.

The rest of us trooped back inside and Paul and I began to clear the table. Lunch had been a strained affair with Dad giving me a lecture about 'the importance of qualifications' and 'a good career meaning a good start in life'. It was so obvious it was aimed at Paul, but I tried to look as if I agreed with everything Dad said. Anything to keep the peace.

Then he started on about how much Paul going to college had cost him. What a waste it all was.

'I will pay you back,' said Paul. 'I really will.'

'It's not the money,' said Dad. 'I want you to be happy.'

'I will be,' said Paul. 'I *am*. I want to see the world. Experience life. It's going to be brilliant.'

'Well, at least let me give you some decent medical supplies for the journey,' said Dad.

Paul sighed. 'It's sorted, Dad. Don't worry.'

Dad didn't look convinced and, for a moment, I felt sorry for him. He doesn't normally look his age but today he did. He looked sad and a touch weary. Sometimes he can't accept that people have their own plans for their lives. He's so used to people obeying his every word at the hospital, he thinks it's going to be the same at home. Poor Scary Dad. I think he means well.

After loading the dishwasher, Mum went to water the pots on the patio and Paul and I went through to the living-room. Paul flopped on the sofa and began flicking through the Sunday papers. At the bottom of the pile was our school newsletter, which he began to read.

'There are loads of things you can do in here,' he said after a while. 'Art, drama, choir. Getting a hobby would be a good way of making new friends.'

'You sound like Dad,' I said, sitting next to him and stretching my legs out on to the coffee table, 'organising my life. Anyway, I have loads of hobbies. Tennis. Football. Karate.'

'Sounds like you'll meet lots of boys doing that stuff, not girls.'

'Don't be sexist. Girls do all that stuff as well.'

'Oh, *sorry*. Didn't realise you're a feminist,' he teased.

'I'm not. I just believe women are the superior race,' I teased back.

'Oh, look, there's you,' pointed Paul as he came across our class photo. 'And Hannah.'

'It was taken just after Easter,' I said, looking over his shoulder. 'I look awful.'

'No, you don't. What are the other girls like?'

'Oh, God. All sorts.' I pointed to some of the girls in the photo. 'That's Melanie and Lottie. I get on OK with them. They were at footie yesterday. Those three are the brainboxes, those two are the computer nerds, Jade and Candice are the bad girls that like to bunk off, Mary and Emma are the sporty girls, Wendy's a bit of a pain.'

'So, who do you hang with?'

'Well, Hannah before she went, obviously. And now, I suppose Melanie and Lottie a bit, but they're a twosome really. I'm lumped in with the brainboxes seeing as I'm usually first in the class at everything. Except maths. I hate maths.'

Paul continued to study the photo.

'Now, she looks nice,' he said. 'Who's she?'

'God, typical,' I said when I saw who he was pointing at. 'She's Nesta Williams. Only the best-looking girl in our school.'

'She looks like that girl in Destiny's Child.'

'Beyonce.'

'Yeah. So who are her friends?'

I pointed out Lucy Lovering and Izzie Foster.

'They look like fun. Tell me about them.'

'Not much to tell. I don't know them that well outside school. They don't do football or any of the stuff I do. Inside school, they're sort of in the middle. Popular. Not too swotty, not too disruptive, though Izzie does ask a lot of questions in class sometimes. One teacher called her Izzie 'why?' Foster. But *everyone* fancies Nesta, that I *do* know. Even Scott next door. She's in the drama group and I think she wants to be an actress. She's probably completely self-obsessed. Anyone as gorgeous as her has to be.'

'Not necessarily,' grinned Paul. 'I'm gorgeous and I'm not self-obsessed.'

'And *I'm* gorgeous and I'm not self-obsessed,' said Mum, coming back in with a bunch of white roses she'd cut. 'So why don't you get in with this crowd?'

'Oh, you don't understand, Mum. They hang by themselves. They'd never let anyone as boring as me in with them.'

'You're not boring,' said Mum, taking the newsletter from Paul and scanning the back page.

'Don't bother to read that,' I said. 'It's completely out of touch and dull.'

'Well, here's your chance to change it,' said Mum, handing it back to me.

'What do you mean?'

'There, back page. I saw it the other day when I had a

look through. I thought you might be interested. It says that they're looking for a new editor, seeing as the old one will be moving on at the end of the year. And they want to make it more of a magazine than a newsletter. Applications open to everyone from Year 9 upwards. You only have to do eight pages or so as an example.'

'Not interested,' I said, putting the newsletter back on the pile of papers.

'But you want to be a writer,' said Paul. 'You should go for it. It would be good practice.'

'Nah, people think I'm a swot as it is. If I went for that, they'd only hate me more.'

'Suit yourself,' said Mum and began to root around in the cupboards for a vase. 'But I see that Sam Denham is doing a talk for all those interested.'

'Sam Denham? Where does it say that?'

'Ah, so suddenly it's not so boring.' Mum picked up the newsletter and read from the back. 'Monday 11 June, 4.30 in the main assembly hall. That's tomorrow. He's going to talk about journalism. It says he got started on his school magazine.'

Sam Denham is a celebrity journalist and though he's old, at least in his thirties, he's still cute in that Ricky Martin kind of way. They always have him on the news when they want an opinion about anything. He always has something interesting or funny to say.

And he's coming to our school?

'Maybe I *will* go to the talk,' I said. 'But only to listen.'

```
email:      Outbox (1)
From:       goody2shoes@psnet.co.uk
To:         hannahnutter@fastmail.com
Date:       10 June
Subject:    Night night
```

Hi Hannah

Feeling mis. Bro Paul gone. He and Saskia are booked on the overnight flight to Goa tomorrow. Boo hoo. Everyone I care about is going away.

Gotta go, school a.m.

TJ

By the way, our crapola newsletter is looking for a new editor and Sam Denham is coming to school tomorrow to do a talk. Apparently, he got started on his school mag.

email: Inbox (1)
From: hannahnutter@fastmail.com
To: goody2shoes@psnet.co.uk
Date: 10 June
Subject: Sam the Man

WAAAAKE UP.

Exscooth me? Did you say Sam Denham as in Sam Denham from the telly? He's a top babe. V V jealous. Wish never left UK. Be sure to wear something short that reveals your legs as they are one of your best features. And sit on the front row.

TJ, you *must* go for editor. You'd be brilliant at it. And it would take your mind off missing me and Paul. I've read all about this kind of thing in Mum's mags. The agony aunts are always telling people to 'keep busy' and 'throw yourself into your work'. I think this is a godsend. Your destiny.

And you think you're miserablahblah? Try being me. In a new country. With no friends at all. Not even Melanie and Lottie. No, young lady, you don't know you're born, as Dad would say.

Yours truly

Your Agony Aunt Hannah

PS: Few more for the book collection
Over the Cliff by Hugo First
The Cat's Revenge by Claude Bottom
Arf arf arf arf arf arf!

Chapter 4

A
Lonely Little
petunia

'I'm just a lonely little petunia in an onion patch, an onion patch, an onion patch,' sang the record in my head. It was going round and round, louder and louder, as I sat eating my lunch in the school playground the next day.

I was on my own because Melanie suffers from awful hayfever and thought that sitting outside would make it worse. Course, Lottie had to stay in with her to keep her company and hand her tissues. I was going to explain that as pollen is airborne, it could get anywhere, so it wouldn't make much difference where she was, but I didn't want her to think I was a Norma Know-It-All. Too many people thought that already. In fact, lately I've found myself holding back when I know the answers to things in class. Let someone else be the one who always gets it right. It doesn't win you any prizes in the popularity stakes.

Perhaps I should have stayed in with them, I wondered, as I looked around at all the groups of friends. It is definitely possible to feel lonelier in the middle of a crowd than when on your own.

Most of the school was out making the most of the heatwave. Everyone in pairs or three or fours. All busy talking, laughing, having a good time. I always used to sit with Hannah at lunch and I felt really self-conscious sitting on my tod. Like, everyone must be staring, going, 'Oh, poor TJ, she's got no mates.'

I continued munching my peanut butter and honey sandwich like I didn't care, but I did care. I didn't like this feeling of being the odd one out.

'Hey, TJ,' called a voice near the bike shed.

I turned round to see Wendy Roberts. 'Hey.'

'You heard from Hannah?' she asked, as she perched herself on the bench next to me and lowered the straps of her top so the sun could get to her.

I nodded. 'Yeah. I've had a few emails. I think she's missing England.'

'You must miss her, too,' she said.

'Yeah, I do,' I replied, wondering what was going on. Wendy never normally gave me the time of day, so why this sudden interest in Hannah? Sensitive and caring are not words that come to mind when I think of Wendy. Mean and self-centred more like. But, no one else had asked about Hannah or how I was, so maybe I'd got her wrong.

'You going to the talk tonight?' she asked. 'Sam Denham?'

I nodded.

'He is gorgeous, isn't he? I saw him on morning telly last week. He was so funny. I wonder if he's got a girlfriend? Are you going to go for editor?'

I shook my head. I wasn't going to tell her, but Hannah's email had made me think. Maybe I *should* go for editor, it would be perfect to take my mind off things, plus, as Paul had said, good practice for when I'm older. But I didn't want to tell Wendy. I didn't want her thinking I was getting ideas above my station and anyway, I might not even get the job.

Wendy got out her mirror and applied some lipstick from her bag. 'Great colour, isn't it?' she said. 'Natural with a hint of gloss. Good for us brunettes. Want to try some?'

'No, ta.' Us *brunettes*? What is all this matey, let's bond over a lipstick act, I wondered. What *does* she want?

'Er, TJ . . .'

'Yeah . . .'

'You know that exercise we had to do for maths . . .?'

Ah. So that was it. I felt my face drop. I couldn't help it. For a split second I thought someone was being friendly because they might have cared about me. Obviously not.

'Well I meant to . . .' Wendy continued.

'You want to copy my homework?' I interrupted.

'Oh, TJ, *could* I? You'd be doing me the most *enormous* favour and you know what Mr Potts can be like if anyone hasn't done it . . .'

'Actually, maths isn't my best subject . . .'

Wendy stiffened. 'It comes so easily to you but if you're going to be precious . . .'

'I'm not. Here take it,' I said and got my book out of my bag. I couldn't be bothered arguing. Maths didn't come easily. I had to really work at it and the last bit of homework had taken hours after lunch yesterday and I still wasn't sure I'd got it right. But I wanted friends not enemies and Wendy could be really nasty when she wanted to be.

Just at that moment I caught Izzie Foster watching me from the bench to my right. She raised her eyebrows and half-smiled at me.

'Thanks. You're a doll, TJ,' said Wendy, grabbing my maths book out of my hand. Off she went, leaving me sitting on my own again.

Izzie was still staring. She was sitting with her mates Lucy and Nesta and, like most of the other groups of girls dotted around the playground, they looked like they were having a good time, just relaxing in the sun. Nesta was at one end of the bench rubbing lotion on to her legs and Lucy was at the other with her skirt hoiked high and her legs stretched out to get the sun. Izzie said something to them and they both looked over, then Izzie got up and came to join me.

'Hey, TJ. I was just thinking. You heard from Hannah?'

'Wendy's already borrowed my homework,' I said.

'What homework?' asked Izzie, looking puzzled. 'I saw you sitting on your own and suddenly remembered that Hannah'd gone. I wondered how you were doing?'

So people *had* noticed me sitting on my own. Well, I didn't need anyone's pity.

'I'm fine,' I said, getting up and putting my half-eaten sandwich in the litter bin. 'Got to go.'

I was going to go and sit and read in a cubicle in the loo for the rest of the lunch break. That way no one would see me on my own and feel sorry for me.

'So, to sum up,' said Sam Denham from the stage later that day, 'you've got five main rules and if you stick to them, you won't go wrong.'

I turned the page of my book to write more notes.

'Rule one,' he said. 'Your job is to stop people just flicking through the magazine. You have to draw them in to actually read what's on the page. You do this by having hooks on the page. These are pictures, titles, words under the picture that give an idea what the feature is about, a quote and the picture captions. Now, if people scan your page, they can quickly access what it's about. So, the title and the captions should be . . . what?'

He looked around as a few hands went up in the hall,

including Nesta Williams' who was sitting next to me. Sam pointed at her to answer.

'*Interesting,*' she said and gave him a flirty smile.

'Right,' said Sam, flashing a big smile back at her and keeping his eyes on her for a few moments. '*Interesting.* Or funny. These hooks are as important, if not more so, than the copy.'

I was scribbling furiously to get it all down when I noticed Nesta hadn't written a thing. 'Do you need paper?' I whispered to her, ready to rip out a page for her.

She grinned and shook her head. 'No, thanks. I'm just here for the view.'

You and half the school, I thought. I don't think a talk had ever been so well attended, not only by the girls but also by the teachers. But then, most of the teachers are aspiring writers, according to Hannah's mum. She was a headteacher before she left for South Africa. She told us that half her staff were secretly working on novels and planning to get out of teaching.

'Rule two,' Sam continued. 'Make sure your picture or photograph is appropriate to the copy. You don't want a big smiley picture of someone next to a tragic piece. Rule three. Use your pictures and captions in a creative way. For instance, you're doing a sports page and have a feature about tennis coaching. Any ideas?'

Wendy Roberts put up her hand. 'You could have a photo of some kids playing, with the caption *Learn to play tennis.*'

Sam nodded. 'You could. It's apt but not very inspiring. Any other ideas?'

I had one, but I didn't want to look a prat in front of everyone. Wendy was blushing like mad after Sam had squashed her idea. I went over in my mind what I'd say if I could only pluck up the courage.

Sam pointed at a girl at the back.

It was Izzie Foster. 'How about a picture of Pete Sampras in full flight going after a ball, saying something like, "Are you the next Sampras?"'

'Now we're cooking,' said Sam. 'That's more like it. Only it might be a bit intimidating, as most people know they'll *never* be the next Sampras. So, it might put them off going. But, good idea. Any more?'

Me *me*, I thought, trying to summon up the courage to put my hand up.

'Come on,' said Sam, looking round at the rows of silent girls. 'Part of being a pro is throwing ideas into the pot and not feeling bad when someone knocks them down. It doesn't matter. We learn as much by our mistakes as our successes, if not more. Come on, who's going to stick their neck out?'

I could feel myself going red as I put my hand up, but I was bursting to see what he thought of my idea.

'You,' said Sam, looking in my direction. 'Lara Croft on the front row.'

I looked behind me. He couldn't mean me, could he? *Lara Croft?* But no one else had their hand up.

He pointed at me again. 'You. Come on. Girl with the plait?'

Oh, he *did* mean me! I could feel myself going redder than ever. I took a deep breath. 'What if you use a picture of, say, Tim Henman?' I finally managed to get out, 'on his backside with the ball bouncing past and a caption saying something like, "even the best needs a little extra help?"'

'Love it,' beamed Sam. 'It may not make you want to play tennis, but it will make you stop long enough to read what's going on.'

'Well done, Lara,' whispered Nesta as the red from my face spread to the tips of my ears.

'Rule four. Never be afraid to try new things. Rule five. In your layout, make sure the reader always knows where to go next. And make sure the information is accessible, especially in a magazine. Know your market. And not too many long paragraphs. Break some of it up. You know, ten tips about this, five ways to do that and so on . . .'

At the end, he took some questions from the floor, but I hardly took in what was going on. I spent the last ten minutes of his talk in a daze at having spoken to him. I was well chuffed that he'd liked my idea. Loved it, in fact. I couldn't wait to tell Hannah later.

As everyone got up to leave, I noticed Sam making his way over to where I was sitting. I froze to the chair. Ohmigod. He was coming over to speak to me. I could feel myself going red again and breathless as I planned what I'd say. I tried my best to look natural and smile as he approached, but I had a feeling I looked like a grinning hyena, I was so thrilled.

As he reached the front row, he knelt down next to me and turned his back.

'So, did you enjoy the talk?' he asked Nesta.

'Oh, yes,' beamed Nesta. 'Fascinating.'

That wiped the smile off my face. Literally. *Fool*, I thought, you utter *utter* fool. He had no intention of coming to talk to you.

I had a quick look round and prayed that no one had witnessed it, but too late, I noticed Lucy Lovering hovering at the side. She'd seen it all. Me perking up with a stupid grin, then Sam turning his back on me to talk to Nesta. God, how humiliating.

I looked away from Lucy and got up to walk out the back door. Sam slipped into my vacant chair as though I'd never been there and continued chatting to Nesta.

'Hey, TJ,' called Lucy, as I reached the school gates and turned into the street. 'Wait up.'

Oh, no. I wanted to get out. Get home and hide. What did she want? I pretended I hadn't heard and carried on walking.

'*TJ*,' said Lucy, catching up.

'Yeah?'

'That was a great answer you gave in there.'

'Thanks,' I muttered and carried on walking. It didn't feel so great any more. 'Bye, Lucy.'

'What bus you getting?' she persisted.

'102.'

'Me too. We can go together.'

'Aren't you going to wait for Nesta and Izzie?'

'Nah. Izzie's gone off to band practice. And Nesta. Well . . .'

'Probably hoping she'll get a ride from Sam Denham,' I said bitterly. I couldn't help it. I felt miffed. Nesta wasn't even interested in writing or going for editor and yet she was the one Sam had picked out for special attention afterwards.

'A ride from Sam?' Lucy giggled. 'That I'd like to see. He came on a bike.'

'Really? I thought he'd come in a flash car or something.'

'I know,' said Lucy. 'But it *is* a flash bike. I saw him arrive on it in a helmet and clips and everything.' Then she added, 'People aren't always how you think they are.'

I felt awkward then and a bit rotten about what I'd thought about Nesta. She can't help being a man magnet.

We stood in silence for a few minutes, then Lucy turned to me. 'I hope you don't mind me saying, but . . . back there, I saw . . . you know . . .'

I shrugged and tried to pretend I didn't care. 'Well, Nesta *is* gorgeous. She has everything any boy could ever want.'

'What? A hairy chest and big muscles?' asked Lucy.

I burst out laughing. 'I thought he was coming to talk

39

to me. Or both of us at least.'

'I know,' said Lucy gently. 'I saw.'

'I felt a right idiot. Like I was invisible or something.'

'I've been there, believe me. I used to feel like that a *lot* when Nesta first arrived,' said Lucy. 'I mean, I know she's my mate, but she is stunning, so people always look at her before anyone else. And she's funny, so people like her. It's easy to feel left out sometimes. I thought she was going to steal Izzie from me when she first began to hang out with us. I thought she didn't want to be my friend, only Izzie's. It was like I wasn't even there. So, yeah, I know *all* about feeling invisible.'

'What did you do?'

'Oh, took a very grown-up approach. Sulked. Acted like a baby. Felt *very* sorry for myself. *Hated* Nesta. Then I got to know her. And discovered that she's really nice. In fact, she had been feeling the same way. She thought *I* hated *her* and didn't want to be her friend.'

Just at that moment, Sam Denham cycled past on his bike and jolted as he went over a bump in the road.

'If you think about it,' said Lucy with a wicked grin, 'men really ought to ride side-saddle.'

I burst out laughing as I watched Sam wobble down the road and disappear round a corner.

'And he did call you Lara Croft,' said Lucy.

'Yeah, he did, didn't he?' I said. I'd forgotten that. 'I thought he meant someone else at first. I guess it's because of my plait.'

'Maybe. But you do have a look of her. So, yeah,' teased Lucy. 'TJ Watts – invisible? Hardly. Only mistaken for the most sexy woman in cyberspace.'

'*Yeah*,' I said. 'Don't mess with me . . .'

I liked Lucy. She was a laugh, like Hannah. She had a way of turning things round and making it all seem OK.

Somehow it didn't seem to matter any more that Sam Denham had snubbed me. He probably didn't even realise he'd done it.

The rest of the journey home flew by as Lucy and I chatted away. As I let myself into the house later, I realised it was the first time in weeks that I'd actually felt happy.

Things were looking up.

---

email:	Outbox (1)
From:	goody2shoes@psnet.co.uk
To:	hannahnutter@fastmail.com
Date:	11 June
Subject:	Wham Bam thanku Sam

Hi H

Excellent talk by Sam Denham. He fancied Nesta, he made a beeline straight for her after the talk.

I am definitely going to go for editor. Hurrah. And thx for the advice.

Got bus home with Lucy Lovering. She's a real laugh and easy to talk to. She has invited me to her house after school on Friday. Brill. Can't wait.

Scott came over to borrow my Buffy vid. He wants to show it to Jessica. He sends his love. He seems to have forgotten he said he'd give me back the money I lent him. I know I should say something, but I can't face it . . .

Got piles of hwk so better go:

Miss you loads

Spik soon

Love

TJ

email: Inbox (1)
From: hannahnutter@fastmail.com
To: goody2shoes@psnet.co.uk
Date: 11 June
Subject: School

TJ

Help. Am mis. Don't like it here. I WANNA come HOME. And now you're going to be best friends with Lucy Lovering and you'll forget me. Started school today. Lots of geeky boys in our class. They have their own language over here. And accent. Like if someone's invited somewhere they say, 'Like, yah, rock up when you like man.' Or 'I rocked up to Jine ee's (Janie's) about farve (five)'. And they say 'och shame' a lot. And a girlfriend is called a 'cherry'. It's going to take me ages to learn it all.

    Gudnight ma cherry

    Spik spox spoooon

    Your v sad friend Hannah. Och shame Hannah.

Mark next door has some book titles for you. As he is a boy, they are all rude or stupid.

    Rusty Bedsprings by I P Nightly

    Chicken Dishes by Nora Drumstick

    And *The Revelations of St John* by Armageddin Outtahere

For Real

'Make yourself at home,' said Lucy, flinging her bag down and opening the fridge.

I pulled a chair out at one end of the pine dining table that took up half the kitchen. Before I could sit, I was accosted by a golden Labrador who appeared from under the table. He put his paws up on my chest and began to lick my face with great enthusiasm.

'*Down*, Jerry,' said Lucy as another dog appeared next to him and joined in the 'let's wash the guest's face' game.

'How many are there?' I asked, wiping my face with my sleeve.

'Two,' said Lucy, opening the French doors. 'Ben! Jerry!' she called as she ran out into the garden. The dogs jumped down and ran after her, tails wagging. Once they were out, Lucy stepped back inside and shut the door. The two dogs looked in through the glass with bemused faces as if to say, 'that was a *really* mean trick'.

'I didn't mind them,' I said. 'I like dogs.'

'So do I. They're my best friends as much as Iz and

Nesta, but they can be a bit much sometimes,' said Lucy, then added with a grin. 'And so can the dogs.'

She held up two cartons of juice. 'Cranberry or apple?'

'Cranberry, please,' I said, settling into my chair. I liked Lucy's house immediately. It looked like the kind of place you could relax in. 'Lived in' as my mum would say. Every surface was covered with books, papers and magazines, the walls were plastered with paintings and drawings and there was a lovely old dresser against one wall with colourful bits of mismatched crockery.

'Hi,' I said to the boy who was sitting at the other end of the table and reading the latest John Irving novel.

'Uh,' he said. Or, at least, that's what it sounded like.

'Steve, this is TJ. TJ, this is my charmer of a brother.'

Steve barely looked up. He only grimaced at what his sister had said.

'Oh, hi TJ,' said Lucy. 'I'm Steve. So *pleased* to meet you. I *would* look at you, but then you are my *younger* sister's friend so why bother? You're too young for me and probably stupid. Nothing you have to say will be of the slightest interest to me. I am your superior in every respect and everything I say, no *think*, will be over your head.'

Steve's mouth twitched. He almost laughed.

'Good book that,' I said, pointing at what he was reading. 'I've read all of his but I liked *The World According To Garp* best.'

Then he did look at me. A strange look as though he was considering something unsavoury that a cat might have brought in. I met his gaze and tried to look friendly.

'New, are you?' he asked.

'Ohmigod, it speaks,' said Lucy, putting a glass of juice beside me. 'Sorry about the juice. It's organic, but it tastes OK when you get used to it. My parents are both health freaks so . . .'

'We have to go out of the house to keep our toxin levels up,' said Steve.

'In answer to your question, no, I'm not new,' I said. 'New here, I guess. But I've been in the same class as Lucy since we began secondary.'

'TJ's a brainbox like you,' said Lucy. 'She's going to go for editor of our school newsletter.'

'Really,' said Steve, looking totally unimpressed.

A brainbox? Was that really how people saw me? How boring.

It got worse.

'She's arm-wrestling champion as well,' continued Lucy, who was oblivious to the fact that I was squirming in my seat. D'oh. Thanks for the great introduction, Lucy, I thought. Like hi, I'm TJ Watts, brainbox with muscles. How sexy is that? Not.

Steve put down his book and did what all boys did when my arm-wrestling talent was mentioned. He put his hand out.

At that moment, the back door opened and another boy burst in and flung his bag on the table. Blonde like Lucy, he looked younger than Steve, maybe fifteen or so, whereas Steve looked like he was in sixth form.

'Excellent,' said the boy, plonking himself down next to me. 'Arm-wrestling. I'll play the winner.'

'TJ, other brother Lal,' said Lucy.

We nodded at each other as Steve and I locked hands and put our elbows down. Steve tried to test my strength before we began. I let my hand go limp in his, so he'd think I was weak. This was going to be easy.

'Ready, steady, GO,' said Lal.

It was all over in two seconds.

'I wasn't ready,' objected Steve, as his lower arm hit the table. 'You called GO too soon.'

'Rubbish,' said Lal, pushing Steve out of his chair and sitting in his place. 'You're a puny weakling. Right. Now me.'

We locked hands and this time Steve called.

'Ready, steady, GO.'

Lal was more of a challenge. Ten seconds.

'Wow. You're pretty good for a girl. Do anything else this well?' he said, picking up my hand and this time stroking it and looking at my mouth with what I can only describe as longing.

Lucy whacked the back of his head. 'Take no, notice, TJ. Lal thinks he's Casanova.'

Lal dropped my hand and Steve did a kind of smirk. 'Don't suppose you can mend computers as well as you arm-wrestle, can you?'

'Maybe . . .' I said.

The rest of the evening went brilliantly.

I fixed Steve's computer no problem. He had one the same make as mine, complete with same operating system. He was well impressed when I pressed a few keys and, hey presto, it worked. He dropped his superior act after that and we got chatting about books. The shelves in his half of the bedroom were heavy with them.

'So who's your favourite author?' he asked.

'God, so many. Can I do top three?'

He nodded.

'OK, I know that they're kids' books but I still love the Narnia books by C S Lewis.'

'Yeah. They're cool,' he said.

'And I like Bill Bryson.'

'Yeah,' said Steve, pointing to his shelf. 'I've got all of his.'

'And I loved *Alias Grace* by Margaret Atwood.'

'How's the computer?' called Lucy from the corridor.

'Mended,' Steve called back.

'Then stop hogging TJ. She's *my* friend,' said Lucy, bursting in the door. 'Come and look at my bedroom.'

I got up to follow her, feeling well chuffed. She'd called me her friend. I hoped I would be. Steve and Lal too. They were all really easy to be with and, for once, I hadn't been tongue-tied when meeting boys.

'Wow,' I said, as Lucy opened the door to her room. 'It's like a princess's room. An Indian princess.'

'Thanks,' said Lucy, looking pleased. 'Me and Mum did it last year. The curtain material is from a sari. I got it in the East End.'

On one of her walls were cut-outs of people from magazines. Not the usual pop bands and actors – I didn't recognise any of them.

'Who are all these?'

'Dress designers. Gaultier. Armani. Stella McCartney. I want to do design when I leave school.'

'Well, I can see already that you have a good eye for colour, Lucy. This blue, lilac and silver looks gorgeous. I wish you'd come and do my room. It's so boring. I think the paint Mum used was called Death by Magnolia.'

'I'll show you some clothes I've made,' said Lucy, opening the wardrobe and pulling out a selection of skirts and tops.

She held some of them up against her and they looked good, even to me, someone who doesn't know a lot about clothes.

'Maybe you could do a fashion piece for my newsletter. Like, what's in for the summer.'

'Sort of five top tips?'

'Yeah. Summer sizzlers,' I laughed.

'Love to,' said Lucy. 'And are you going to change the name of the newsletter? *Freemont News* sounds *sooo* boring.'

'Exactly what I thought. I *was* going to change it. What

do you think of calling it *For Real*?'

'Brilliant,' said Lucy, 'because that's exactly what it isn't at the moment and it's *exactly* what everyone wants. You're going to be so good at this, TJ. I can tell already that you're going to win.'

I shrugged. 'I'll give it a go. But I was amazed to find out how many others are going for it after Sam's talk.'

'I know,' said Lucy. 'Even stinky Wendy Roberts, though she was mega-miffed after Sam didn't go for her answer. I saw her face at the back. She was livid. Even more so when he loved yours.'

'She's even more mad with me today. She borrowed my maths homework and I'd got most of it wrong. Not my fault if it's my worst subject.'

'Serves her right,' said Lucy as the doorbell rang downstairs. 'Don't worry, one of the boys will get it. Probably Nesta, she said she'd come over.'

Sure enough, Nesta appeared moments later.

'Hey,' she smiled at both of us and flopped on the bed. She looked slightly surprised that I was there, but not unduly bothered. The whole evening was going so well. Maybe I could be friends with her too?

'We were just discussing the newsletter,' said Lucy.

'Cool,' said Nesta. 'So, you going to go for it?'

I nodded. 'And Lucy's agreed to do a fashion piece.'

'Excellent,' said Nesta. 'And I tell you what readers like more than *anything*. A make-over. You know, before and after sort of thing.'

'Good idea,' said Lucy.

Nesta was staring at me. 'And you know who we should do?'

I shook my head.

'*You*, of course. You could look *fabulous* if you wanted to.'

Lucy looked shocked. 'Nesta. TJ *does* look fabulous. Honestly, you and your big mouth. You don't think before you open it, do you?'

'What? *What*?' said Nesta, looking flustered. 'I didn't mean anything . . . I only meant . . .'

I tried to smile but I wanted to die. She thought I looked awful. I knew I didn't wear all the latest fashions, but she didn't have to rub it in. I got up to leave.

'Oh, don't go, TJ,' said Lucy.

I looked at my watch and made for the door. 'I have karate at seven and it's the last one before the summer hols, so I can't miss it. Honest, really, it's OK.' I did my best to look cheerful, but Lucy didn't look convinced.

'TJ, I hope I didn't . . .' started Nesta. 'Oh, hell. I mean . . . I was only trying to say, I don't think you make . . .'

'Nesta. Button it,' said Lucy, linking my arm. 'Come on, I'll show you out.'

When we got to the front door, Lucy made me promise I'd come again. 'You sure you're OK?' she asked.

I nodded. I wanted to get away. And I did have karate that night, not that I was in the mood any more. I really wanted to go home and talk to Hannah on email.

I looked back at Lucy's house after she shut the front door. No way was I going to go there again for Nesta to point out how awful I look. It's all right for her, she'd look fab in a bin-liner.

---

email: Outbox (2)
From: goody2shoes@psnet.co.uk
To: hannahnutter@fastmail.com
Date: 15 June
Subject: Best friends

To Hannahnutter
I was so wrong about thinking I could be mates with Lucy. Not in a million years. Not while she's friends with Nesta Williams. You won't *believe* what she just said . . . That I need a make-over. So everyone at school pities me. And thinks I'm a swot. And ugly. Everything over here is awful.

I called Scott to ask if he could think of anything I could do to improve my appearance. He laughed and said, you could wear blue more often, it will go with your veins. He thought it was really funny. I said I was upset and needed cheering up and he said he'd phone me back after watching 'Friends'. He hasn't phoned back yet.

I miss you loooooaaaaads. Spik spoon.

TJ

From: goody2shoes@psnet.co.uk
To: hannahnutter@fastmail.com
Date: 15 June
Subject: Where are you?

Hannah. *Where* are you?

   Even Scott hasn't phoned me back and he promised.

   And Paul will be on the other side of the world now.
Probably on some amazing island like in *The Beach*.

   I feel so alone.

   Love TJ

Oh, I met Lucy's bros tonight. They're sweet and the eldest
one Steve is OK when he drops his snotty act. He gave me
some brill book titles and suggested I put them at the back
of the school magazine as a sort of silly fun page.

   Bubbles in the Bath by Ivor Windybottom

   A Stitch in Time by Justin Case

   Chest Pain Remedies by I Coffedalot

   Skin Rash Remedies by Ivan Offleitch

   WHERE ARE YOU? I have to go to sleep now as it's late.

Furry Friends

I woke up the next morning feeling better. It was the weekend and Mum had promised to take me to Battersea Dogs' Home. Who needed girlfriends? I was going to get my new best friend of the furry kind.

I got dressed and hurtled down the stairs. Nobody in the kitchen. No one in Dad's study. No one in the living-room.

'Where's Mum?' I asked, on finding Dad sitting out on the patio reading the paper and having a cup of coffee.

'She got called out on a case. Good morning, TJ.'

'Oh, yeah. Morning. Good. When will she be back?'

'She couldn't say . . .'

'Oh, *no!*' I wailed. 'We were going to go to the dogs' home. And I have football this afternoon . . . We won't have time if she's not back soon.'

'I've got the day off,' said Dad. 'Ready when you are.'

'School all right?' asked Dad, as he drove down Edgware Road towards Hyde Park.

'Yeah.'

'Not long until the summer holidays?'

'No. Not long.'

'Feeling all right?'

'Yeah. You, Dad?'

'Yes. Fine, thank you.'

I could see that he was trying, but I wasn't in the mood for telling him how I was really feeling. He'd never understand how much I missed Paul and Hannah and what it was like to be the only girl in Year 9 without a best friend. Plus, I didn't want to get him started on Paul and how he's wasted his opportunities. The last thing I wanted was a lecture on how I must focus on school and my career and get good grades.

I felt relieved when he gave up and switched the radio on, even if it was to listen to classical music. He means well, does Dad, but sometimes, he's so busy offering his solutions that he doesn't realise that he hasn't really listened to the problem. It's much easier to talk to Mum. She understands better that sometimes people don't want to be told what to do, they just want someone to listen and give a bit of sympathy.

I spent the rest of the journey looking out of the window as we drove down Park Lane, towards Victoria then over the Chelsea Bridge.

'I've always wanted to come here,' said Dad, as we parked the car near Battersea Park. 'I've been wanting a dog for *ages*.'

'Really?' I said as we got out and walked round the corner to the Home. 'I never knew that. Have you ever had a dog before?'

Dad nodded. 'When I was a lad. Best friend I ever had. Being an only child, he was my constant companion.'

'What was his name?'

'Rex.'

'What happened to him?'

'He died after I left for university. I was heartbroken. I thought it was my fault, you know, because I'd gone away and left him. But my mother said it wasn't like that. She said it was his time to go and that he'd waited until I'd gone so as not to upset me.'

We walked into the reception area at the home and I watched Dad as he found his wallet to pay our entrance fee. I swear his eyes misted over when he'd talked about Rex. It made me see him in a new light. Dad clearly had a soft side when it came to animals.

'Pound for you,' said the lady behind a counter. 'And fifty pence for the young lady. Have you come to look or to buy a dog or cat?'

'Buy a dog,' I said.

'Then you need to have an interview with a Rehomer first. Follow the red paws on the ground and someone will come and talk to you. See what sort you want and so on. Then you follow the blue paws and go and have a look.'

I couldn't wait and felt really excited. I could see Dad

did as well. He'd turned from Scary Dad into Smiley Dad.

We followed the red paws and went to sit in the waiting room with a group of other people. A sign on the wall told us that it cost £70 for a dog and £40 for a cat. After a short wait, a man in a red tracksuit came out and called us into a room where he asked loads of questions about where we lived and whether there were other children or cats and if was there a garden.

It was funny because he was stern like a headmaster and Dad had to really sell the fact that we would be good owners.

'Our chief concern,' said the man, finally relaxing, 'is that the dogs go to a permanent home where they will be happy and well cared for – for the rest of their lives. Hence the interrogation. Many of our dogs are here because their previous owners couldn't or wouldn't care for them. Last thing we want is for a dog to have another bad experience.'

'Quite right,' said Dad. 'I can assure you that we'll take very good care of whoever we get today.'

'OK, then. Let's go and look at the dogs,' said the man.

Dad looked at me and winked as we followed the man along the path of blue paws through a courtyard to a building at the back.

Inside it was like a hospital with long sloping corridors leading up to different floors. Each corridor had a different name: Oxford Street on the ground floor where the clinic was; Bond Street and Bow Street on the first floor where the dogs were kept; Regent Street and Baker Street on the second with dogs and cats and a private floor, Fleet Street and Pall Mall on the top.

'Here we go,' said our Rehomer, opening a door to a side ward. 'I'll leave you to look around. Take your time, then, when you've decided, we'll bring the dog to you for an introduction and see if you get on. Takes about fifteen minutes. Then, if all parties are happy, you can go.'

Two things hit us as soon as we entered the ward. The sound of barking. And the smell. Not a bad smell, but distinctive nonetheless. Like wet hay mixed with dog food.

'*Phworr,*' I said.

'Aromatherapy of the canine kind,' laughed Dad, as we looked in to see the first hopeful face looking out at us from behind bars.

'It's like they're in a prison cell,' I said as a Jack Russell poked a paw through at us and barked in friendly greeting.

We spent the next hour walking through all the wards on every floor. We must have seen about fifty dogs. Each one had a little room in which was a blanket, water, a toy and outside access to a corridor at the back.

There were all sorts of characters to choose from. Collies, Beagles, Jack Russells, mongrels of every colour even a Samoyed, which Dad told me was a rare breed. He looked like a big white teddy. At the side of each cage was a report with the dog's details: the breed, name, age, history and whether they liked cats or children. Whether they needed an experienced owner and whether they were destructive or not!

At the end of their report was a comment as though written by the dog. 'I make a good companion.' Or 'I need commitment.' Or one big dog whose comment said, 'I am a majestic individual!'

'That one sounds like you, Dad,' I said, pointing at the last one. With his tall stature and silver-white hair, Dad did have a majestic air.

'I don't know what you mean,' he laughed, then pointed at one that said, ' And there's one that sounds like you – "I have a strong will and need a lot of training".'

On one ward, a black mongrel called Woodie was doing everything he could to get people's attention. All sorts of mad antics – bouncing off the walls, paws up against the bars. It was as though he was saying 'pick me, *pick me*, look what I can *do* . . . back flips, jumping, bouncing!!!! Pick me. *Pick me.*'

Another old brown–and–white collie sat looking at us with pleading eyes. She looked as though she had a bad wig on.

'This is heartbreaking,' said Dad, reading her report. 'She's called Kiki. She's thirteen.'

Kiki put her paw through the cage and even though there was a big sign saying not to touch the dogs, Dad took her paw and stroked it. 'Hello, girl.' Then he turned to me and I swear his eyes were misting over again. 'Poor thing. At her age, she's probably here because her owner died or something. She looks as though she's been well looked after though. Shame, because a lot of people come here and only want the young dogs. They see "thirteen years" and see the expense of vet's bills.'

I was finding it excruciatingly difficult. I wanted all of them. Every ward we went into, the dogs would perk up and start wagging their tails as though Dad and I were their best and oldest friends. So pleased to see us. It was like they were saying, 'Oh *there* you are, hold on a mo, I'll just get my stuff and we can go.' Then, as we walked past their cages, their faces would fall and their tails would go down as if thinking, 'Come back. Hey, where are you going? I thought we were outta here?'

'Can't we hire a coach, Dad, and come back with it and say right, everyone in? And then go and buy a big house in the country . . .'

'I wish,' said Dad. 'But, sadly, we can only have one. Have you made up your mind?'

I shook my head. I'd fallen in love with about six of them. Woodie and the Samoyed and Kiki the old collie, a mongrel that looked like an old teddy, a beautiful black Alsatian and a cheeky Jack Russell.

Some had to be overlooked as it said clearly on their report that they could be destructive and didn't like children, even teens. Others, I knew, were too big like the Alsatian. Arm-wrestling champion that I am, I knew I wouldn't be able to keep him on a lead.

It was then that I turned a corner and saw Mojo. He was sitting quietly in his room, a medium-sized black dog with a white patch over one eye. He gazed up at us with the saddest eyes I've ever seen. You look how I felt last night, I thought. Sad, lonely and badly in need of a friend. 'Mojo is four years old and a stray,' said his report. 'He has a very gentle nature and likes people. He is very distressed at finding himself here and would like a good home as soon as possible.'

Mojo looked up at me with hopeful eyes.

I glanced over at Dad.

'He's The One, isn't he?' said Dad.

I nodded.

Dad and I didn't stop talking all the way home. He told me all about how he had wanted to be a vet, but didn't think he could cope with having to put people's pets down as you sometimes had to do.

We even talked about Paul.

'At least this fella won't get on a plane and leave us,' said Dad, looking at Mojo who was sitting happily in the back, looking out of the window. 'Unlike some people I could mention.'

'Paul, you mean?'

Dad nodded. 'I hope he's all right, wherever he's got to. He may be grown-up, but you never stop worrying. And I know you and Mum think I go on but I know my own son and he can be naïve at the best of times. Even as a young lad, he was a dreamer, too trusting of people . . . You have to have your wits about you when you're travelling.'

'He'll be OK,' I said. 'He's with Saskia.'

'Hmmmph,' said Dad. 'And she's as daft as he is. Still, I guess he's not alone. You're right.'

I was glad it had been Dad who'd come with me to the Home. I felt I'd got to know him better. And discovered he was missing Paul as much as I was.

When we got home, Mojo ran around sniffing everything. Tail wagging happily, he seemed more than pleased when Dad opened the French doors to the garden. He ran out and sniffed the air as if he couldn't get enough of it.

'I think he likes it here,' said Mum, watching him from the kitchen. As he ran about familiarising himself with the smells, the phone rang.

'Oh, that will be someone called Lucy again. She's phoned a few times since I've been back and so has someone called Nesta.'

I went to answer the call. Mum was right. It was Lucy.

'About Nesta last night,' she said. 'She really didn't mean to upset you. What she meant to say was that with your potential you could look totally amazing. She wasn't saying you looked awful or anything.'

I'd forgotten all about the incident the night before. And it didn't seem so bad in the light of a new day.

'I suppose I *was* being a bit over-sensitive,' I admitted. 'Overreacted a bit.'

'We all have days like that,' said Lucy. 'Like my mum says, only the wearer of the shoe knows where it rubs. You know, sometimes we don't know where each other's sensitive spots are and tread on them by mistake. Nesta treads on people's sensitive spots with hobnailed boots on. But she doesn't mean to. We all want to be friends. Honest. We all agreed. That's why Nesta came to sit next to you at Sam's talk the other afternoon.'

'Really? I thought that was just coincidence.'

'No. It was so you had someone to sit with.'

'Really?'

We chatted on for about ten minutes and I told her my news about Mojo. She wants to come over on Monday to meet him.

After I put the phone down, I had plenty to think about. It looked like I had misjudged the whole situation and I decided I should give Nesta another chance. I watched Mojo as he ran about. He looked a different dog already. His tail was wagging madly, his tongue out.

Mum had her radio on in the kitchen and an old song was blasting out. How true, I thought, as I listened to the lyrics. 'What a difference a day makes, twenty-four little hours . . .'

We're all going to be good friends, I thought, going out into the garden to Mojo and doing what I'd wanted to do ever since I'd set eyes on him.

I gave him a big hug.

email: Inbox (1)
From: hannahnutter@fastmail.com
To: goody2shoes@psnet.co.uk
Date: 16 June
Subject: Asta la vista

Ola bamboo baby.

Me velly sollee no email back last night.

   Sollee you had bad time. Wish I was there to make it all better. Confucius, he say all things will pass. Particularly if you eat plennee fibre. Arf, arf.

   Had brill time. Went for a grand beano feast and drinky drunky woos at a girl from school's. She's new like me only she's come here from Johannesburg (known over here as Jo'burg). I think we might be friends. Her name's Rachel.

   Am getting bronzed and beautiful. It may be OK here after all.

   She has two book titles for you. Bit rude.

   Poo on the Wall by Hoo Flung Dung

   Dog Bites by R Stornaway

   Love you loads

   Hannah

email: Outbox (1)
From: goody2shoes@psnet.com
To: hannahnutter@fastmail.com
Date: 16 June
Subject: Illo mysterio of lifeio

Great to hear from you. All changed from last night. V happy. Have new furry friend called Mojo. He's adorable and Mum says he can sleep in my room. I think Dad is jealous. He was so sweet today at the dogs' home. I realised I don't know my dad as well as I thought. He's v worried because Paul said he'd call when he got to Goa but nothing so far. Hope he's OK. I think it's just Paul and he'll call when he remembers.

Also, Lucy called and apologised about Nesta. May be OK after all but no one will ever replace you. I am glad you met this new girl though as I don't want you to be lonely. Lucy said her bro Steve liked me and thought it was unusual to meet a girl who had half a brain and was good to talk to. Not sure if this is a good thing as boys seem to view me as 'one of the lads' and I would like to have a boyfriend some day. Maybe Nesta was right. Maybe I do need a make-over. Anyway, I told Mum I want to change my appearance and maybe try and look a bit more like a girl. She was v pleased and said I can have a new dress.

Scott came over to meet Mojo. He has ditched Jessica already. He was looking mucho cute and was very sweet with Mojo.

Funny business, life, isn't it? Just when you think everything's rotten and life stinks, it can all change.

Love you.

TJ

Books:

Rhythm of the Night by Mark Time

Bad Falls by Eileen Dover

email: Inbox (1)
From: paulwatts@worldnet.com
To: goody2shoes@psnet.co.uk
Date: 17 June
Subject: Goa

Hey TJ.

In Goa, it's awesome. We sleep under the stars and look out over the sea. We met some amazing people (travellers mostly – Brits and Irish and a large number of Dutchies) and the locals here are very kind. I have bought an amazing crystal and every time I hold it, it is like there are enormous beams of light pulsating through my head via my temples, brow and crown chakra, but it gives Saskia a headache. I have been having real funky lucid dreams lately and been feeling like a million dollars with this quartz.

Rock on.

Paul

PS Please let Ma and Pa know I am OK. Tried to ring but lost wallet soon after we arrived. Have got job in a bar though. So all OK. Please ask Ma to send some dosh. Tell her I'll pay her back, promise, promise. Don't mention to Dad. Saskia got some nasty insect bites. Please ask Ma to send some more homeopathic stuff – arnica and apis and citronella and lavender oil.

Dog
of the Week

Our class was in a mad mood the next week at school. I think the heatwave had affected everyone's brain.

It started in science, when Mr Dixon asked if anyone knew the formula for water.

Gabby Jones put her hand up. 'HIJKLMNO,' she said proudly.

'Er, can you tell me why?' he asked.

'Yesterday, sir,' said Gabby, 'you said H to O was the formula for water.'

'H_2O,' he sighed, then wrote on the board. 'H_2 as in the *number* O. OK, last question about water. What can we do to save water in a water shortage?'

'Put less in the kettle sir,' said Lucy.

'Excellent. Anyone else?'

'Don't use the hosepipe,' I said.

'Another good one. Any others to help our water supply go further?'

Jade Wilcocks' hand shot up. 'Dilute it, sir,' she said.

Mr Dixon shook his head but I could see he was trying not to laugh.

Then it was into the school hall for a film about the cosmos and all the planets and stars. Afterwards, Miss Watkins asked us questions to see if we'd been paying attention as I think some girls used the hour in the dark as an excuse to have a kip.

'What is a comet?' asked Miss Watkins.

I knew the answer to this and put my hand up.

'Star with a tail, miss.'

'Correct. And can anyone name one?'

Candice Carter, who was one of those I saw nodding off, stuck her hand up. 'Mickey Mouse, miss,' she said, as everyone cracked up.

But the best was in RE. Again, it was poor Miss Watkins taking the class and she asked if anyone knew what God's name was.

This time it was Mo Harrison who put her hand up.

'Andy, miss.'

'Andy? Why on earth would Andy be the name of God?'

'It's in all the hymns, miss,' said Mo. 'Andy walks with me. Andy talks with me . . . There are loads of examples.'

'No, Mo,' Miss Watkins said, turning to Nesta who was crying with laughter. 'Nesta Williams, seeing as you clearly find it so funny. What do *you* think the name of God might be?'

'Er, not sure,' said Nesta, looking caught out. 'What do you think?'

'I don't think,' said Miss Watkins. 'I *know.*'

'I don't think I know either,' giggled Nesta.

The whole class got detention but it was worth it. I felt like I'd spent the whole morning laughing my head off.

We never did get to know what God's name was.

'How are you getting on with the mag?' asked Izzie as we sat doing our lines in detention in the lunch break.

'So-so. I've got some ideas, but need to get them down on paper,' I replied.

'Come over to ours at the weekend,' said Lucy. 'I'm sure Steve would like to see you again and he can help. And so could me and Izzie and Nesta.'

The offer of help was tempting. Less than two weeks to go until the entries were due in and there was going to be a lot of competition. Intense discussions and hushed conversations were going on everywhere.

'I could do a horoscope page for you, if you like,' said Izzie.

'That would be brilliant,' I said. 'And I may do a piece about Battersea Dogs' Home.'

I showed Lucy and Izzie the Polaroids of Mojo. Soon, everyone wanted to look, so they got passed round the class. Everyone ooed and aahed until it got to Wendy Roberts.

'Arrr, *sweet,*' she said loudly. 'TJ's new boyfriend. Hey, TJ. Is this *all* you can pull? He needs a bit of a shave.'

A few girls giggled half-heartedly, but as though they felt they had to rather than because they thought Wendy was hilarious. Why was she being so horrid to me? Was it because Sam had liked my answer and not hers? Or because she'd got a low mark after copying my homework? It wasn't my fault I was crapola at maths. I racked my brains for something funny to say back so it would look like I didn't care, but I couldn't think of anything quick enough. Bummer and bananas, as Hannah used to say. Why can I never come up with the right words when I need them?

After detention, we all trooped out to the playground for the last ten minutes of lunch. I ate my sandwiches and stretched out in the sun, but I couldn't help but notice that some girls were passing a piece of paper round, then staring at me and giggling in a nervous way.

Oh, what now? I thought, as Izzie came out to join me on the bench.

'What's going on?' I asked.

'Oh, Wendy. You know she's running for editor as well. She's just jealous . . .'

'Take no notice,' said Lucy, coming to join us. 'You don't need to know, TJ. She's a sad cow and you should ignore her.'

'No, I want to see,' I said and got up and went over to a group of girls who were standing round Wendy looking

71

at the piece of paper. I glanced over Wendy's shoulder. There was a picture of a dog with its head cut out and mine stuck on instead. She'd cut out the photo of me from the group shot in last month's newsletter. Underneath Wendy had written 'Dog of the Week'.

'What do you think, TJ?' giggled Wendy. 'You getting your dog gave me the idea. Each month in the newsletter, we pick someone to be Dog of the Week. What do you think?'

As I searched for the right put-down, a voice behind me got in first. 'I think, Wendy, that if you were any more stupid, you'd have to be watered.'

I turned round and there was Nesta. She looked mad.

She took the paper and, much to Wendy's astonishment, she ripped it up. 'This is not remotely funny, Wendy. And you know it's not. It's not journalism. It's just nastiness. Come on, TJ. Don't lower yourself by breathing the same air as this low life.'

I was as gobsmacked as Wendy, but I turned away with Nesta and followed her to a bench where Lucy and Izzie were sitting.

'Thanks, Nesta,' I said, 'but I was OK. I can handle Wendy Roberts.'

'I know. But I've been waiting for a chance to show you that I'm on your side. I'm sorry about the other day. Sometimes words come out the wrong way.'

'Not just then,' I grinned. 'That was brilliant. I wish I could come out with stuff like that. I always think of good things to say later, like when I'm falling asleep or something . . .'

'Nesta's special talent is fighting for her mates,' teased Lucy. 'Her special downfall is her big gob.'

'Well, I know what it's like to have some saddo like Wendy have it in for you,' said Nesta.

'I don't know why. I never did anything to her.'

'With her sort you don't have to,' said Nesta. 'She's probably jealous.'

'Of me? Don't be mad.'

'Looks and brains,' said Nesta. 'Lethal combination.'

I felt really chuffed. Maybe she didn't think I looked too bad after all.

Then I looked over at Wendy who was glowering at us from the other side of the playground. I hoped this wasn't going to be the start of something.

Then I looked at Lucy, Izzie and Nesta glowering back at her like they were my best mates. And I hoped that this *was* going to be the start of something.

```
email:        Outbox (1)
From:         goody2shoes@psnet.co.uk
To:           hannahnutter@fastmail.com
Date:         18 June
Subject:      notalot
```

Dear H

Weather is lovely. Wish you were here.

TJ

```
email:        Inbox (2)
From:         hannahnutter@fastmail.com
To:           goody2shoes@psnet.co.uk
Date:         18 June
Subject:      notalot either
```

Dear TJ

Weather is here. Wish you were lovely. Arf arf.
   Must dash. Going to movie. ie. Drive-in.
   Bigola hugs and heeheehasta la vista baby.
   Hannah

   Book title:
   Chest Complaints by Ivor Tickliecoff

From: nestahotbabe@retro.co.uk
To: goody2shoes@psnet.co.uk
Date: 18 June
Subject: Friday night

Hey, Lara Croft

Wanna come to a sleepover Friday night? Iz and Lucy are coming. About 7?

Nesta

Sleepover **Secrets**

'TJ. TJ!' called Mum excitedly as she came in the door. 'Where are you?'

'Here,' I called from upstairs where I was straining to get started on some ideas for the school magazine. So far, I'd written one word. Aggh.

It was Friday night and I was going to the sleepover at Nesta's in half an hour. An evening of culture had been planned. 'The Simpsons' and 'Buffy' on Sky then 'EastEnders', 'Friends' and 'South Park'.

Mum came in carrying a large carrier bag and plonked herself on the bed. She looked *very* pleased with herself.

'I couldn't resist,' she said, getting something wrapped in tissue out of the bag. She pulled out a calf-length dress with swirly rust, maroon and orange-coloured flowers on it.

'What do you think?' she asked.

The word 'disgusting' came to mind, though I suppose

it was pretty in that cottage-chintzy-curtain-fabric way.

'Not your *usual* taste, Mum,' I said, thinking I was being diplomatic. Mum isn't fashion-conscious at the best of times but her style is more plain than flowery. Jaeger and Country Casuals for work and sloppy tracksuits for the weekend. And her idea of making an effort to dress up is to wear a blue glass bead necklace. Even if it's with the tracksuit.

'Not for me, silly,' said Mum. 'It's for *you*.'

Whaaat? Aggggh. No. *Buuuut it's horrid*, I thought.

'It's lovely, isn't it? I saw it in a little boutique opposite the surgery and remembered what you'd said about wanting to look more like a girl. Perfect, I thought. I described you to the lady in the shop, said you had dark hair and hazel eyes and she said you'd be an Autumn according to her Colour Me Beautiful chart and would suit the brown rusty colours,' said Mum, not drawing breath. 'Cost a fortune but we won't tell Dad. It's about time you had something nice. So what do you think?'

She was so delighted with her purchase that I didn't have the heart to hurt her feelings.

'There aren't words,' I said truthfully.

'I *knew* you'd love it. You can wear it to your new friend's house, can't you? Try it on, try it on.'

I smiled weakly as I desperately searched for something to say. Hmm? *How* do I get out of this one?

Ten minutes later, I was in the kitchen wearing the dress

and still wondering, literally, how to get out of this. Course, that had to be the very moment Scott banged on the back door.

'Evenin' all,' he said, letting himself in and stroking Mojo, who jumped up in greeting. Then he saw me. 'Yuk. You going to a fancy dress?'

'*Shhh,*' I said. 'Mum's upstairs. She bought it for me.'

'What, to wear?'

'No. To scare off burglars. *Yes*, to wear.'

Scott pulled a face. 'You look weird. Like you're in "The Waltons".'

'Thanks a bunch. So how do I get out of it?'

Scott went round to my back, put his hands on my waist and nuzzled into my neck. 'Now *that's* one thing I'm good at, helping girls out of their dresses.' He started to stroke my hair then play with my zip. 'Now, Miss Watts,' he whispered. 'I really don't think this is your style. Let me help you out of it and into something . . . more . . . comfortable.'

I giggled and slapped him, hoping he didn't see me blushing. Him nibbling my neck made me feel all fluttery inside. Nice.

'*Uhyuh yunnawee,*' I started to say, then took a deep breath and made myself remember this was Scott *for heaven's sake*. 'Seriously though,' I said, turning so he couldn't see my red face. 'I'm going to a sleepover tonight at a new mate's house and I can't possibly wear this. She'll think it's so naff.'

'What new mate?'

'Oh,' I suddenly remembered he fancied Nesta. 'Er . . . Nesta Williams new mate.'

'You're kidding. *Nesta?* Why didn't you tell me? When did this all happen? I thought you said she was an airhead.'

'Well, I was wrong. She's actually very nice.'

Scott punched the air. '*Yes.* Will you promise, promise, *promise* to put a word in for me? Or even better, you could bring her here and I could kind of casually drop in and you could introduce us?'

I *could* I suppose, I thought, watching Scott as he went into the hall and checked himself in the mirror. I just wish that a boy would feel that enthusiastic about me one day. And even more to my surprise, I found myself thinking, I wish *Scott* would feel that enthusiastic about me.

By the time I was due to go, I had a plan.

I went down into the kitchen wearing my usual tracksuit and trainers to find Mum chopping peppers and onions on the counter.

'I can't wear the dress tonight, Mum. I'm going via Lucy's house and they've got two huge dogs. Labradors. *Very* hairy. *Always* moulting. The kind of dogs who jump up on you. With *enormous* claws and muddy paws and they like to chew everything. They'd *ruin* my dress. Do you mind if I put it away for a special occasion?' (Special occasion like Bonfire Night and I put it on a guy to be burnt, I thought.)

'Sure,' said Mum. 'And are you *sure* you like it?'

Was she giving me a get out? I was about to open my mouth and say *nooooo*, I hate it . . .

'Because they had it in pink,' she said.

Ag. Agh. Agherama.

Later, I thought, as I made for the door. I will sort this later.

'Got your jimjams?' asked Nesta, closing the front door behind us. She looked fab in a lilac cami set with the words *Groovy Chick* across the top.

I nodded as she led me through into a living-room with high ceilings, deep-red walls and plush brown velvet sofas. Impressive, I thought, as I took in the mix of dark wood and Turkish and Moroccan-looking rugs.

Izzie and Lucy were already there, curled up for our telly night and both gave me a wave. Izzie was wearing red flannel pyjamas with fluffy sheep on and Lucy had blue ones with stars and moons all over. I waved back and hoped that they couldn't see how nervous I was feeling. Nesta's flat was so glam, I hoped they wouldn't think my house was mega-dull when they came to visit me.

'You can change in there,' said Nesta, showing me a cloakroom off the hall. 'No one's here. Tony's staying over at a mate's and Mum and Dad have gone out to eat. Mum said we can order pizza. What's your fave?'

'Four cheeses. Please,' I said, as I closed the cloakroom door behind me.

'Coming up,' called Nesta. *'Quattro formaggi.'*

My pyjamas looked so boring as I got them out of my bag. A pale grey vestie thing for the top and bottoms to match. Ah well. What you see is what you get, I thought, as I pulled them on, then went back into the living-room and pulled a cushion on to the floor.

'Let the viewing commence,' said Izzie, passing me the Pringles.

After we'd finished watching 'South Park' and munching our way through crisps, pizza, chocolate and ice cream, the real fun began. Nesta put on a *Riverdance* video. After we'd danced our socks off for fifteen minutes, we all collapsed on the sofa and they talked about *everything* – music, clothes, mags, school gossip, horoscopes and, finally, boys.

As they chatted, we painted each other's toenails. I did Nesta's dark purple and then she did mine the same colour. Izzie did Lucy's pale blue and she did Iz's red. None of them seemed to mind that I didn't say a lot. I was happy to sit back and take it all in.

Nesta was a hoot and seemed to be *very* experienced with boys. She's had loads of boyfriends. At least eight. Maybe more, I lost count. And she seems to be an expert on snogging.

Izzie is just fab. She's into loads of interesting stuff, not just horoscopes but alternative health, food, nutrition, aromatherapy, crystals and witchcraft. And she's *also* in a band with her boyfriend. His name's Ben and the band's called King Noz. She sang a song for us that she'd written herself. She has the most amazing voice.

And Lucy. Lucy's sweet. And kind. She kept checking on me to see I had enough to drink and eat. And was I comfortable. Did I need another cushion?

They all made me feel so welcome I suppose it was inevitable that, in the end, they'd turn the spotlight on me.

'So TJ, is there anyone you fancy?'

I shook my head. 'Not really.'

'So why've you gone red?' asked Nesta.

'Nesta!' said Lucy.

'What? *What?*'

'Let her tell in her own time,' said Izzie.

I decided to plunge in. They'd all been so open with me, I felt I should be the same with them.

'Well, I suppose there *is* one boy,' I said. 'I've known him all my life, but he treats me more like one of the lads than a girl.'

'Does he know you fancy him?' asked Lucy.

'*Noooo*. In fact,' I said, looking at Nesta, 'he fancies you.'

'*Me?*'

'Yeah, he's seen you at the Hollywood Bowl and asked if I'd put a word in.'

Nesta looked surprised. 'What's his name?'

'Scott Harris.'

'Don't know him,' said Nesta. 'And anyway, I have a boyfriend.'

'Posh boy,' teased Lucy.

'Simon Peddington Lee,' said Izzie in a voice like the Queen's.

'He's away at school at the mo,' said Nesta, 'but we speak or text most days. He'll be back soon for the summer hols. And, *anyway*, I don't steal other girl's boyfriends.'

'He's not my boyfriend.'

'Not *yet,*' said Nesta. 'Anyway, you saw him first so in my book that means he's yours whether he knows it or not.'

'Maybe you should let him know you like him,' said Iz.

'*Noooo*. Can't. *No*. You don't understand. That would ruin everything. See, he's one of the few boys I can talk to. I have known him so long I don't get all tongue-tied like I do around boys I fancy.'

'You got on with my brothers OK,' said Lucy.

'Yeah. But that was different.'

'Ah, you don't fancy Steve. Is that it?'

'No. Yes. I don't know. I didn't think about it. It felt so natural round your house, I kind of forgot he was a boy. And, well . . . it's just, we got off on the right foot. I won at arm-wrestling and we were away.'

'Got off on the right arm then,' grinned Lucy. 'Not foot.'

I decided to tell them everything. 'See, I can karate-chop a boy to the floor and stand on his neck easy peasy, but the thought of having to kiss one and I'm terrified.'

'*Ah* . . .' said Lucy. 'I get it.'

'You have to be like Buffy,' said Izzie. 'Like, one minute she's snogging Angel, the next, she's out vaporising vampires. It's a question of balance.'

'Right,' I said, feeling more confused than ever.

I could see Nesta was bursting to say something.

'What?' I said.

'Nothing,' she said, but she was holding her stomach as though keeping something in.

'Spill. I can take it.'

'No. Nothing. Well. What if . . .? No . . . nothing . . .'

'Oh, for God's sake, Nesta. Spit it out,' said Izzie.

'Well,' said Nesta. 'How about you don't tell Scott you fancy him? How about we get him to fancy *you*?'

'Ah,' I said. 'And how do you propose to do that?'

I knew exactly what she had in mind, but felt like teasing her.

'Er, . . .' she looked anxiously at Lucy. 'Dunno really.'

I decided to help her out. 'You still want to do a make-over, don't you?'

'Er, *no*,' she said with a quick glance at Lucy.

'You think I look like a bag lady, don't you?'

'*NO*. I never said *that*!' Now Nesta looked really worried. Lucy may be small in height but she's clearly big in Nesta's books. 'No. *No*. I think you look fab. Oh, all right . . . I think you could look fabber. With a make-over. That's all. And now you're going to hate me. And think I'm mean because I want to help. And Lucy's going to go on about my big gob. And how I never know when to stop . . .'

I laughed. 'I'm only teasing you. No, please, do it. To tell the truth, I took a look at myself in the mirror this evening in the dress from hell that my mum bought me and I thought, TJ, you need help. I'd love it if you gave me a make-over. I'll use it in the magazine. And . . . anyone got a pen? I've had an idea for a feature for the mag. A Sleepover Special Report.'

Nesta handed me a pen and paper from the drawer in the desk behind the sofa. Then she took my face in her hands and turned it to profile and back. Then she clapped her hands and went into drama luvvie persona, 'A mi-vake over. Oh, *daaahlling*, ve're going to mi-vake you look *faaaabulouse.*'

D'oh, I thought. What've I let myself in for?

Sleepover Special Report

Ever wondered what makes the perfect sleepover? *For Real* asked four teenagers for their top tips and fave ingredients. Here's what they came up with.

Five main ingredients
1) Nosh for the munchies
2) Drinks
3) Videos & DVDs
4) Music
5) Make-up for make-overs
6) Mags

Special Spot Report

Izzie Foster. 14. Aquarius. Finchley. London
Fave thing to do at sleepovers? Goss. Listen to music. Nosh.
Fave music for sleepover? Anastacia. Christina Aguilera.
Fave video? *Austin Powers 2*. Yeah baby yeah.
Top nosh? Choc-chip cookies. Doritos.
Top drink? Organic elderflower juice.

Nesta Williams. 14. Leo. Highgate. London
Fave thing to do at sleepovers? Dance. Read problem page in mags and have a good laugh. Make-overs.
Fave music for sleepover? Destiny's Child. Craig David.
Fave video? *Charlie's Angels* or *Scream*.

Top nosh? Nettuno pizza with extra cheese. Häagen Dazs.
Top drink? Coke.

Lucy Lovering. 14. Gemini. Muswell Hill. London
Fave thing to do at sleepovers? Talk about snogging and boys.
Fave music for sleepover? Robbieeee.
Fave video? *Titanic*. I'm King of the Wooooorld.
Top nosh? Chinese take-away. Yum. Pecan nut Häagen Dazs.
Top drink? Hot chocolate made with milk and marshmallows.

TJ Watts. 14. Sagittarius. Muswell Hill. London
Fave thing to do at sleepovers? Chill. Laugh my head off.
Fave music for sleepover? *Top of the Pops* summer CD.
Fave video? *South Park Christmas Special* starring Mr Hankey
the Christmas Poo.
Top nosh? Burger and chips. Toffee popcorn.
Top drink? Banana milkshake with vanilla ice cream on top.

Chapter 9

American
Pie

'So The Plan is,' said Nesta, through a mouthful of toast, 'we all go to TJ's and sift through her wardrobe.'

It was Saturday morning and we were still in our jimjams, sitting round in the kitchen, eating toast and drinking milky coffees.

I wondered if I could get out of The Plan. Not that I was bothered about the make-over any more, no, I was worried what the girls were going to make of the Wrinklies. Izzie, Lucy and Nesta's parents were normal ages. And Nesta's are so *glamorous*. I met them this morning while I was waiting for the bathroom. Her mum's a newsreader on cable television and her dad's a film director and both *très* good looking and stylish as far as grown-ups go.

Mainly though, I was worried what the Wrinklies might make of the girls. Dad in particular. He can turn into Scary Dad at the slightest bit of noise or disturbance.

Our house was never one to throw its doors open and welcome in the neighbourhood. I always used go to Hannah's house rather than the other way round. Dad likes his privacy, the fewer people he sees when he's not working, the better. Radio 4 and peace and quiet and he's happy. Last thing I wanted was him showing me up in front of new friends by asking them pointed questions like, 'What time's your bus home?'

I thought I'd better warn the girls.

'OK, er, about my parents, well my dad . . .' I said and explained the situation.

'Same at our house,' said Izzie. 'My mum doesn't exactly encourage me to bring my mates back. Some parents are like that. It's easy to hang at Lucy's or here where no one's running round cleaning up after you all the time.'

'So, no problemo, TJ,' said Nesta. 'We will be the perfect example of quiet refined teenagers.'

'Well behaved and demure,' said Izzie.

'And *very* mature,' said Lucy.

I breathed a sigh of relief. I could trust them to be cool. At that moment, the back door opened and Leonardo DiCaprio's younger Italian brother walked in. I mean, this boy was *seriously* handsome.

'TJ, Tony. Tony, TJ. My brother,' said Nesta as if I hadn't realised.

'Hi, TJ,' said The Vision.

'Hi, Tony,' said a friendly voice inside my head.

However, what came out of my mouth was, *'uhyuh'*. Oh, *noooo*, I thought. Alien Girl from the Planet Zog is back to haunt me.

Tony looked at the croissant I was about to eat, then looked right into my eyes and did a half-smile that made him look even more gorgeous. 'So, TJ, what do virgins eat for breakfast?'

'Dunno,' I replied, breaking his gaze and staring at the floor.

'Thought so,' he said and laughed.

'Take no notice of Tony, he's a dingbat,' said Nesta. 'So. Aren't you going to ask?'

'Ask what?'

'How come Tony is my brother?'

'No.'

'Why not?' asked Nesta. '*Everyone* asks. He's light-skinned, I'm dark-skinned, how come?'

'Obvious,' I said. 'Same father, different mothers.'

'Hmmm,' said Nesta. 'Smart cookie.'

'Not really,' the voice in my head said. 'I met your mum and dad this morning. I know she's Jamaican and your dad looks Italian. Tony looks like your dad so I reckon he must have had a different mother. Elementary, my dear Williams.' However, Noola the Alien Girl is a person of few words and all that came out was, '*uh*'. Smart cookie indeed. Why did this *always* happen when boys I fancied were around?

'My real mum died before I knew her. I was six months old,' explained Tony, coming over and laying his head on my shoulder. 'Really, I'm an orphan. An orphan prince who needs *love* and *affection*.'

'*Uhyuh*,' I stuttered, hoping that by some strange quirk of fate, Tony might be fluent in Zoganese.

I could see Lucy giving me a strange look then giving Tony a *filthy* look. Hmm? Something going on there, methinks. Must ask later.

Tony went over to the fridge and opened the door. 'What's to eat?' He got out a half-eaten apple pie, put it on the breakfast bar and cut himself a huge slice.

'Apple pie for breakfast?' said Iz. 'Ew. Gross.'

He turned and grinned at her. 'Would you prefer I did something else with it?'

'Like what?' said Iz.

'You seen that film *American Pie*?'

'Yeah,' said Izzie, then pulled a face. '*Eew*, double gross.'

'What are you on about?' I asked.

Nesta looked at Tony wearily and sighed. 'Sorry about my disgusting brother, TJ. In *American Pie*, a boy asks what it's like to have sex. His mate says it's like putting your thingee in a warm apple pie.'

I blushed furiously as Tony watched me closely to see my reaction.

'Apparently, some guy in Australia tried it,' said Lucy, getting down from her stool at the breakfast bar and refilling the kettle. 'Steve read about it in the paper. This guy didn't wait for the pie to cool when it came out of the oven. He was taken to the local hospital and treated for burns.'

'A*ggghhh,*' said Tony, putting his hands over his crotch as the rest of us cracked up laughing. 'I wonder how he explained *that* to the nurse on duty.'

Lucy looked at the apple pie and I saw a wicked twinkle appear in her eye. 'Would you like me to warm that up for you, Tony?' she asked sweetly. 'I could put it in the microwave. On high?'

Tony went over to her and put his arm round her. 'And how *is* the love of my life?'

'Dunno. How is she?' said Lucy as she took his arm away from her shoulder.

'You know you want me really,' said Tony.

Lucy began to walk out of the kitchen. 'Yeah. Right. It's *agony* keeping my hands off you. Not.'

'That girl . . .' Tony sighed as he watched her go out of the room. 'So what are you lot doing today?'

'Make-over,' said Nesta.

'Who's the poor victim this time?'

Nesta looked at me. I looked back at the floor.

Tony got up and started dancing in front of me. 'Don't go changing, tryin' to please me . . .'

'Go and see Mum, Tony,' said Nesta. 'It's time for your medication.'

'So what was all that about?' I asked Lucy. The four of us were sitting on the bus on our way over to my house later that morning. 'You know, Tony?'

Lucy shrugged. 'We used to go out. Then we finished.

Then we got back together. I don't know where we are now.'

'Muswell Hill,' teased Nesta, as the bus went up the Broadway past *Marks & Spencer*.

'He adores you,' said Izzie.

'That's part of the problem,' said Lucy. 'See, we're just getting on great, then he starts again . . .'

She caressed the air with her hands . . . 'with wandering hands. I'm not ready for all that yet. I want it to be special when I go further with a boy. I don't want to do it because I feel pressured that if I don't, he'll dump me for someone who puts out more easily. You know?'

I nodded. No, I didn't know. I hadn't even been *snogged* yet.

'And you saw what he's like,' said Lucy. 'Flirting with you . . .'

'Oh, I never . . .' I started. 'I would never . . . I mean he *is* gorgeous, there's no denying that, but . . .'

'Oh, don't worry, TJ, he's like that with all girls. That's another reason why I don't give in to the wandering hands. I'd never feel as if I could trust him.'

'Well, no reason to worry about me. You saw what I was like back there. Always the same when there are decent boys around. I told you, I go *stupid*. You know there's that book *Men are From Mars, Women are From Venus*. Well, I want to write one, *Men are From Mars, Women are From Venus, Teenagers are From Planet Zog*.'

'Good idea,' said Lucy.

'It's mad,' I continued, 'because, I want to be a writer

but, well, I told you my problem with finding the right words at the right time. Why do they always come after, like when I'm falling asleep or something?'

'That's good, it means your subconscious mind is working on it,' said Izzie. 'I find that with my lyrics. You have to consider the words. Play with them until you've got them right. Let them come to you sometimes. It can happen in the middle of the night. I'd say that is the sign that you *will* be a writer.'

'And if you're from Planet Zog,' said Lucy, 'you can always write science fiction.'

I laughed and punched her arm. 'I wish I could be more like you, Nesta. I wish I could come out with great one-liners or put-downs.'

'*We* all wish she'd be more like *you*,' said Lucy with a grin. 'Think before she speaks, sometimes.'

'It does get me in trouble,' said Nesta. 'Sometimes.'

'So, at last,' said Lucy as we got to our gate. 'We get to meet the man of the moment.'

'Who? Scott?' I said, glancing up at his bedroom window to see if he'd seen us. 'He usually goes out Saturday mornings.'

'No, silly. Not Scott,' said Lucy, pointing at the downstairs window next to our front door where a furry face was looking out. 'Mojo.'

I laughed as I unlocked the door and was almost knocked over as he leapt up to say hello.

'I've only been away a night,' I said, as he licked my face then ran round the girls, sniffing then rolling on the floor, his tail wagging madly.

After they'd all made a huge fuss over him, we all trooped up to my bedroom.

'Fab garden,' said Nesta, looking out of the window. 'It's huge and *wow*, a hammock. How cool. You've got visitors though. On the patio, your gran and grandad are here.'

I went over to look out.

'Er, no,' I said, pulling back. 'That's my mum and dad.'

Nesta looked like she wanted to die.

'Mum had me late, when she was in her mid-forties.'

'Oh, *très* Cherie Blair,' said Izzie, going for a look.

'No,' said Nesta. '*Très* Jerry Hall. Much more glam. Now let's look in your wardrobe.'

And that was it. No problem. *Très* Jerry Hall and show us your clothes. I needn't have worried at all.

'I hope I didn't offend you,' said Nesta as she held up baggy tracksuit bottoms and put them on the reject pile. 'You know, calling them your grandparents.'

'No prob. I know they're ancient. In fact, I call them the Wrinklies.'

'I nicknamed my step-father The Lodger when he first arrived,' said Izzie, flopping on the bed next to Mojo. 'I couldn't relate to him any other way, although we get on better now. But the thought of him sharing a bed with Mum, you know, *eew* . . .'

'Huh,' said Lucy. 'You think you've got problem parents? Mine get the prize. Why can't they be normal instead of mad hippies? They're so embarrassing sometimes.'

'My brother's a hippie. You know the one who's abroad. I could introduce him to your mum and dad when he's back.'

'Yeah,' said Lucy. 'They could have a soya bean party or something and talk about vegan shoes.'

'Vegan shoes?' I asked.

'Plastic. No leather. Dad sells them at the shop.'

'I think your mum and dad are great,' said Izzie. 'I really like them.'

'Well that's because you are a *very* strange person,' said Lucy.

Izzie retaliated by throwing a cushion at her.

Not wanting to be left out, Nesta grabbed one of my pillows and bashed both of them over the head with it. 'Oh, be*have*,' she said in her best Mike Myer's voice.

Both of them picked up cushions and began pelting her.

If you can't beat them, join them, I thought as I reached for a second pillow.

It was hysterical. Even Mojo joined in, jumping on whoever he could and barking his head off.

Five minutes later, Lucy was face down on the floor with Izzie sitting on her back. Izzie was tickling her under her arms. 'Repent, repent. Say I am the most fab fabster in the world, no, the *universe*.'

'Never,' cried Lucy into the carpet.

Whilst they battled it out on the floor, Nesta and I were using my bed as a trampoline.

'I'm Xena, Warrior Princess,' cried Nesta as she leapt in the air and whacked me over the head with a pillow.

'And *I'm* Buffy the Vampire Slayer,' I yelled as I delivered a nifty whack to her knees. '*Die*, you pathetic imbecile.'

Just at that second, my bedroom door opened.

'What in *heaven's* name is that din?' shouted Dad above the racket. 'It sounds as if someone's being murdered.'

We all froze on the spot as if playing a game of statues.

Dad was definitely in Scary Dad mode and I prayed he wasn't going to make a scene.

'Aren't you a bit old for this tomfoolery?' he asked.

Nesta and I got off the bed and Lucy and Izzie got up off the floor. We stood in line, looking sheepish and not knowing what to do next. Lucy was staring at the floor, Izzie was grinning at my father like an idiot and Nesta was looking at her nails, trying to pretend that she wasn't there.

Then I noticed Lucy's shoulders going up and down in silent laughter. This set me off. Then Izzie. Then Nesta, as all of us exploded into a fit of laughing.

Dad looked to the heavens in exasperation. '*Fourteen*, TJ. Isn't it about time you started acting like a young woman?'

I nodded furiously, but tears were falling down my cheeks.

'I'm going to my club for a bit of *peace*,' said Dad, going out and slamming the door behind him.

'Oops,' I said, then started sniggering. 'Iz, Lucy, Nesta meet my dad. Oh dear . . .'

'Sorrysorry,' said Nesta. Then she picked up one of my bras from a pile of ironing on the desk and put it on over her T-shirt.

'Guess we're going to have to work on our refined and well behaved bit, huh?' she said, sticking her chest out.

I nodded. 'Demure and wotsit,' I said, picking a pair of knickers from the pile and putting them on my head.

'And vewee vewee mature,' said Lucy in a little girlie voice as she sprang up on my bed and jumped up as high as she could.

email: Inbox (4)
From: hannahnutter@fastmail.com
To: goody2shoes@psnet.co.uk
Date: 22 June
Subject: Cape Town boy babe

Mambo bandana baby. Bin bisy bee. Fabola barbie last night and I have neeews. I met a boy. I seriously think he may be the One. I may even have to phone you for a yabayaba. He is Drop Dead Divine. A bronzed Adonis. His name is Luke. We had devine tucker and deep talk.

H X

PS Luke (swoon swoon) has a book title for you.
Romantic Fantasies by Everly Night. Heehee. Double arf.

From: hannahnutter@fastmail.com
To: goody2shoes@psnet.co.uk
Date: 22 June
Subject: Scary Dad

Where are you? I phoned and got Scary Dad who said you were at a sleepover. Then he grilled me about whether my mum and dad knew I was phoning. Don't dare phone again. Get thine holy finger out and email me as SOOON as you get in. Loooooooooaaaaaaaaaaads to tell you.

Hx

From: hannahnutter@fastmail.com
To: goody2shoes@psnet.co.uk
Date: 23 June
Subject: Alert alert. Lost TJ Watts.

Okela. Ista no joke no more. *Ou est* you? *Ou Ou OU?*

Hx

From: paulwatts@worldnet.com
To: goody2shoes@psnet.co.uk
Date: 23 June
Subject: hols

Hey, little sis. Hope it's all going well and Scary Dad not giving you too hard a time. Life here is truly wonderful. Did a day with a holy man, amazing as he is out here in India, but is really from Kilburn. Lots of stuff happening with my third eye. Plus he's re-energised my chakras.

Did two-day meditation session with holy man. Nice group. All gelled well. Fairy-story landscapes and sunsets. Friendly people but Saskia has got amoebic dysentery.

Rock on. Stay true.

Paul

PS Please can you ask Ma to go to the Embassy and get me a new passport. Mine was nicked when I slept on the beach the other night. Ta. Plus some peppermint oil and sulphur and pulsatilla homeopathic stuff for the runs.

From: goody2shoes@psnet.co.uk
To: hannahnutter@fastmail.com
Date: 23 June
Subject: Friday night

Hey H

Glad you met boy. Luke. I want *details*. Height? Weight?
Snogged yet? Level of snogging? Marks out of ten for
snogging? etc.

Me had fabola time at sleepover with Nesta, Izzie and
Lucy. Nesta's bro is divine, but taken by Lucy. Sort of. He
has wandering hands apparently, which Nesta says is a
disease a lot of boys in North London suffer from. She's
going to do a make-over on me for the magazine.
Before/after kind of thing. They all came over to go
through my wardrobe but couldn't find anything. *Quelle*
surprise. Oh and Mum bought me the dress from hell. Lucy
said I had to be honest with mum so I was and she's given
me the receipt so I can change it. Thank de Lord. After
we'd been through my wardrobe, we went into the garden
as we are having uno heatwave here. It was nice and relaxed
as Dad had gone to his club for A BIT OF *PEACE*. (He
caught us being *un peu* silly and making a lot of noise and
well, you know what he can be like.) Nesta had a go on the
hammock under the cherry trees. Scott came running over

the minute he spotted her from his bedroom window. He leapt over the fence with a flower, trying to impress her, but he gave her the shock of her life and she fell out of the hammock. Then Mojo jumped all over her. It was very funny. Scott was all over her, all dopey with big cow eyes. I felt a bit jealous, although I know that she has a boyfriend and she said after that Scott wasn't her type. Still. I wish a boy would be all over me. I think I may be the only girl in our class who hasn't been snogged. Maybe I'll never get a boy ever. Maybe I'm just not the sort boys like.

TJ

---

email: Inbox (1)
From: hannahnutter@fastmail.com
To: goody2shoes@psnet.co.uk
Date: 23 June
Subject: you don't 'alf talk rubbish sometimes

TJ

You're not the only girl who's never been snogged in Year 9. I know for a fact that Joanne Richards and Mo Harrison haven't been and unless Mo sorts out her halitosis, she never will be.

Luke. Height 6ft at least. Blonde. Body like a god. Snogged yes. Level 3. OK, 4. Well, he is a god. Marks out of ten for snoggability? 9. But practice will make perfect.

I think it's great, those girls doing a make-over. You are gorgeous, but don't make the most of yourself. I've always said this. I like the sound of Nesta, Iz and Lucy and often thought that if I hadn't been friends with you, I would like to have been friends with them.

Tata for now

Hannah. South African goddess of luurve

Books: Are you still doing this?

Run to the Loo by Willie Makeit

My
Fair Lady.
Not

'You'll never do it,' I said, beginning to feel desperate. 'It's hopeless. I am Ugly Git from Uglygitland.'

'Roma wasna builta in a day,' said Nesta, tugging her way through my hair.

'The darkest hour is just before dawn,' said Lucy, who was kneeling on the floor next to me, retouching my nails.

'Suppose,' I said, looking gloomily at my reflection in the mirror in Nesta's bedroom. My hair was a frizzy mess, I had an aloe vera face mask on that made me look like a ghost and a big spot threatening to erupt on my chin.

'Lack of self-esteem,' said Izzie. 'That's your problem, TJ. You are a babe, but you don't know it. Look, you have fabulous hair that you always scrape back in a plait, long *long* legs that you never show, a fab figure that you hide in baggy tracksuits and a great mouth that all those thin-lipped models who have collagen injections would die for.'

Always one to accept compliments graciously, I said, 'Humphh. And you clearly have the observational skills of a brain-dead gnat.'

We'd already done the 'before' shot in the morning at Lucy's house. Steve had offered to be photographer with his new camera and it was hysterical. I'd worn the 'dress from hell' that Mum had bought me and Izzie had done my hair in two bunches high on either side of my head. Lucy had stuck dog hair from Ben and Jerry's brush on to my legs with Evostick so that I'd look like I had hairy legs (I put my foot down when she got carried away and tried to stick some on my upper lip to give me a moustache though.) And Nesta had given me some lessons in bad posture so I looked even more frumpy.

'All beautiful women have great posture,' she'd said. 'It's one of the first things they teach at modelling school. To stand up straight. So for these shots, stoop, like you have round shoulders.'

Lucy raided her mum's jumble sale bargain bags and produced some seriously tasteless jewellery. Big dangly earrings and an Indian necklace.

'But they don't go with the dress,' I'd said.

The girls had looked at me as if I was stupid.

'And the object of this exercise *is*?' said Nesta.

By the time they'd finished, I looked like a sack of old potatoes. With hairy legs.

'You look awful,' Steve'd said approvingly when I came down the stairs, then walked across the hallway like a duck. A round-shouldered duck.

'Yeah, like Waynetta Slob from Harry Enfield's show,' laughed Lal.

'I want to do the shots round the back garden near the bins,' said Steve.

'What, like I'm on the scrap heap?' I asked.

Steve gave me a look as if to say 'yeah', then he grinned. 'You don't look that bad,' he said. 'It's only that dress that makes you look like a frump.'

'But the bins in the background give a sort of subliminal message, like I'm a load of rubbish,' I said.

'Yeah,' said Steve. 'Exactly. We've been doing it in film class, all about how surrounding images register with the subconscious and can reinforce what you're trying to say without people realising.'

'What are you on about?' said Lucy. She did an enormous yawn as though bored out of her mind, but I found what he was saying interesting.

We had a great laugh as Steve clicked away and I assumed the most unattractive positions and facial expressions I could.

At one point, Mr and Mrs Lovering came out to see what we were up to. They watched for a moment as I cavorted for the camera doing my sumo-wrestler position, then a bit of karate chopping. They looked very puzzled to hear Steve say in a French accent, 'And look as miserable as you can. Like your durg 'as just died and gone to durgee 'eaven *avec les autres chiens*. That's it. *Eh bien. Marvelleuse mon ooglee légume . . . Diable* mon sooth, chins up, chins down. *Mais oui, bien sûr. Degoûtantamont.*'

Clearly languages were not his thing, I thought, as his parents both shrugged and went back into the house.

The second part of the make-over wasn't a laugh. Oh no-ho, not at all. The girls were taking it seriously. As in *mega-seriously*. They were on a blooming make-over mission.

I was plucked, waxed, massaged, moisturised, conditioned, manicured, pedicured, blow-dried, made-up, made-over and dressed.

'OK, you can look now,' said Nesta, removing her dressing gown from the mirror where she'd draped it so I couldn't see.

The reflection of a brunette Barbie doll gazed back at me. I was wearing one of Nesta's dresses, a short pale blue number and her mum's Jimmy Choo grey strappy heels. Nesta had given me 'big' hair, loose and flowing over my shoulders and Lucy had made up my face with a little shadow, blusher and rusty lippie.

'You shall go to the ball, Cinders,' said Nesta. 'You look fab.'

'Yeah, a top babe,' said Lucy. 'Do you like it?'

I wasn't sure. I did look good. And I had to admit that

my legs looked really long. But I wasn't sure that looking like such a girlie girl was me. Mind you, I didn't know what *was* me.

'What do you think, Izzie?'

'Watch out boys,' she sang. 'There's a new kid in town.'

Nesta's mum gave us a lift to Hampstead High Street where we were meeting Steve to do the 'after' shots.

She dropped us halfway down Heath Street and as we got out of the car, someone did a long wolf whistle. I looked over to where it was coming from and there was Scott. He was with a bunch of his mates sitting at a table outside Café Nero.

'TJ Watts. *Cor* bloody cor,' he said, as he looked me up and down and then up and down again, his eyes finally resting on my legs. 'You're a *girl*.'

'*Uhyuh,*' I said, as I noticed all the other boys round the table also oggling me. I felt exposed standing there in my shorter than short dress and I wasn't sure I liked the attention I was getting. Everyone was staring and there was nowhere to hide. Even an old bloke in his forties was gawping as he went by. Served him right, I thought, when he walked smack into a woman with her dog and got all tangled up in the lead.

Scott took my hand and introduced us to his friends. He seemed to be enjoying himself immensely. Then he was all over Nesta and acting like he'd known her for ever. All his mates sniggered when she dismissed him saying, 'In your dreams'.

He didn't seem to mind though. In fact, I think he took it as a come-on.

Lucy spotted Steve coming down the street and waved. He waved back and, when he saw me, he did a slow whistle under his breath.

'See they've done a number,' he said.

'Wow,' I said to Izzie as we walked or rather they walked and I tottered. 'Is it really this simple? A bit of lippie, high heels, show your legs and boys turn to jelloid?'

Izzie nodded. 'And even more so if you show a bit of cleavage. It's amazing to watch. Hysterical. You see boys' cheekbones twitching with the effort not to look at your chestie bits, but their eyes keep zinging back there as if pulled by an invisible magnet.'

'Not a problem I have,' said Lucy, 'being a 32 triple A myself.'

'Lucy's bros call her Nancy-No-Tits,' confided Nesta.

'We can't all be Dolly Parton like you,' laughed Lucy, punching her arm.

We went down to the bottom of Heath Street with Scott and his mates trailing after us and sat at a table outside House on the Hill. Nesta ordered drinks and Steve took some shots as he said he wanted them to look natural rather than posed. This time I didn't have to do much, he did all work. He was much quieter this time, not acting as loony mad as he had been in the morning. He wasn't as much fun. In fact, he seemed to want to get it over with, as though he'd lost interest.

'Why did you choose Hampstead for the "after" shots?' I asked, in an attempt to get him talking.

'Trendy place. It's glam. Rich,' he said, then he clamped up again.

He didn't hang around after he'd got his photos and muttered something about having to get back to finish homework.

Something had clearly upset him since this morning. He was really subdued. I must ask Lucy if she knows.

email: Outbox (1)
From: goody2shoes@psnet.co.uk
To: hannahnutter@fastmail.com
Date: 24 June
Subject: The new *moi*

Hey Hannahlooloo

Had brill time today with make-over. Steve took photos on his new camera. Will send copies. Nesta made me look very girlie girl but not sure it's me. Felt uncomfortable for a few reasons. I never realised before that you can be invisible in big baggy clothes and no one takes too much notice. It's kind of safe. But going out in Hampstead today, everyone was staring. I felt exposed. Nesta said to 'strut my stuff, girlfriend', but people act differently to you if you do. Girls can be bitchy. Boys disturbed. Scott went all googly-eyed at me. But mainly people stared. I wasn't sure if I liked it. Talking of which, we bumped into Wendy Roberts coming out of Accessorize. She did a double-take when she saw me and almost spat out her Magnum. Then she said that dressed like I was, I should go far, the further the better. I wasn't sure what to make of her reaction.

   Spika soon
   Love TJ

PS Yes, yes. More book titles, as I'm definitely going to put some in the mag. *Body Parts* by Anne Atomy

email: Inbox (2)
From: hannahnutter@fastmail.com
To: goody2shoes@psnet.co.uk
Date: 24 June
Subject: The noo *vous*

Ole *le* noodley noodles baby

I think the word to describe Wendy's reaction is *envy*. God, I wish I'd been there to see her. And you. I do miss Hampstead and Highgate and hanging out. I bet you looked the business. Don't worry about looking girlie. You'll find your style. Today was just the beginning of TJ as Sex Queen of North London. Remember Confucius he say, every journey start with first step. That is, unless step going sideways or backwards.

Have been to Luke's posh pad *avec* pool this weekend. Some consolation for missing Ingerlandie.

May your flobbalots be mighty

HannahXXXXXXXXXXXXXXXXXXXXXXXXXXXXXXXXXXXXXX

From: hannahnutter@fastmail.com
To: goody2shoes@psnet.co.uk
Date: 24 June
Subject: d'oh. Steve?????

Er exs*cooth* me?? But I just re-read your email. Have you been holding out on me? More about Steve? Details? Height? Weight? Fanciability? Etc etc.
Immediatetment.

Hannah

---

email: Outbox (1)
From: goody2shoes@psnet.co.uk
To: hannahnutter@fastmail.com
Date: 24 June
Subject: d'oh. Steve?????

Gordy flobbalots. I told you already. *Lucy's* elder brother. Fanciability. I guess he's nice-looking, but not in a drop-dead way like Scott, who I think I may be in love with. And at last he's noticed I am a girl. It's different with Steve. He's easy to talk to. I don't go peculiar when he's around. He's a mate.
   TJ

Book: *Strange Breasts* by Won Hung Low

email: Inbox (1)

From: hannahnutter@fastmail.com

To: goody2shoes@psnet.co.uk

Date: 24 June

Subject: d'oh. Steve?????

Zoot allors. Snog him anyway and get in some practice!

HXXXX

Book: *Drink Problems* by Imorf Mihead

Walking the Durg

'Don't go into the woods,' said Mum, as I got ready to take Mojo for a walk on Wednesday after school. 'Stay on the roads where people can see you.'

'I'm going to ask if Scott will come,' I said. 'Then it will be OK, won't it?'

'Yes, fine,' said Mum. 'But don't be too late back. You've still got homework to do.'

I couldn't wait to call on Scott. I'm sure it wasn't my imagination that he'd been so flirty in Hampstead on Saturday. He'd seemed genuinely bowled over by my new look and at one point he'd held my hand and squeezed it. I'd got that lovely fluttery feeling again, like when he'd nuzzled my neck. I couldn't stop thinking about it and what it might be like to hold his hand again and even kiss him. My insides went all liquidy and peculiar just imagining it.

I combed my hair loose, put on a bit of lippie, then put

Mojo on his lead and went next door.

Mrs Harris answered.

'Is Scott home?' I asked, trying my best not to give away the fact I was quaking. Mad really, as I'd been over to his house a million times and thought nothing of it.

She called up to him in his room and he emerged at the top of the stairs a few minutes later.

'Oh, hi TJ.'

'Er. Hi. Um. I'm taking Mojo for a walk. Do you want to come?'

He shook his head. 'Watching "The Simpsons",' he said.

'Oh. OK, cool. Another time,' I said, hoping that I hadn't shown how disappointed I was. He didn't even come down to say goodbye.

As Mojo and I went up to Muswell Hill Broadway I wondered if I'd misread the signals. Had he ever held my hand before? Or squeezed it? I couldn't remember. Maybe I was reading too much into it. Maybe he hadn't liked my new look after all. But he seemed to at the time. He kept staring at me. I felt so confused.

I decided I'd look in a few shop windows in the hope of finding an alternative style to Barbie babe. Fat chance, I thought, as I looked at the various tops and skirts on display. I wasn't sure what I wanted to look like, though one thing I was certain about was that I didn't want to wear those high heel things again. Agony. They may have looked good, but there was only so far I was prepared to go in the 'have to suffer to be beautiful' game.

Mojo trotted alongside me happily as I pondered the great philosophical question of who was the real TJ Watts.

Is she Noola the Alien girl?

Or Miss Strop-Bossy Prefect who likes to put boys straight?

Or Arm-wrestling Champion of North London?

Or Miss Goody 2 Shoes who always does her homework?

Or Norma Know-It-All?

Or Barbie's brunette sister?

Or on the other hand, is she a total nutter with loads of different characters living in her head?

'What do you think, Mojo?' I asked as we made our way past the cinema and down Muswell Hill High Road.

'Aha,' said a voice behind me. 'Talking to yourself, first sign of insanity.'

I turned and there was Steve with Ben and Jerry.

'I was talking to Mojo,' I said. 'But you might be right about the insanity bit. In fact, I was just thinking I might well be going bonkers.'

He laughed. 'You going to Highgate Woods?' he asked as Mojo, Ben and Jerry got down to the dignified business of sniffing each other's bottoms.

'No,' I said. 'Mojo would love to, but Mum said I mustn't go on my own.'

Steve checked his watch. 'Well, we have just been, but I've no doubt these guys wouldn't object to a bit longer. Come on, I'll keep you company.'

I gave Mum a quick ring on my mobile and, after giving me the third degree, she finally agreed.

We set off for the woods and once inside, let the dogs off their leads. They raced off excitedly, best of friends already. As they charged about, Steve and I chatted like old mates. It's so weird, I thought, here's me all great pals with Steve and nervous with Scott, whereas only a week ago, Scott was my pal and Steve was a complete stranger.

'So, what's with you and that guy?' asked Steve after a while.

'What guy?'

'One outside Café Nero. You seemed to like him.'

'God, am I *that* obvious?' I was taken aback that he'd read my thoughts. 'I hope he didn't notice.'

'I don't think he did. Too busy ogling Nesta.'

My heart sank. Maybe that was it. It was really Nesta he was interested in. And he'd been doing the flirty bit to get to her through me.

'I know,' I said. 'He lives next door to me. Has done for years and we've always been mates. Until lately. It's all changed. I found myself . . . you know, er, well, thinking about him a lot. I don't know what I feel, it's all so weird. And I certainly don't know what he thinks, but I don't think he rates me other than someone to talk to. Oh, I don't know . . .'

'Any boy who doesn't fancy you must be mad,' said Steve. 'And I'll tell you one of the biggest secrets about boys . . .'

I held my breath for the great revelation.

'They're exactly the same as girls in that they also feel shy and awkward that they don't always say the right thing or act the right way.'

'Really?'

Steve looked at me closely. 'Boys may act confident, but can be just as nervous as you underneath. Everyone fears being turned down and looking a fool.'

'I just don't think he's interested . . .'

'How do you know who's interested or not?' said Steve. 'Sometimes when a boy is acting disinterested, it's actually more frozen than cool. Frozen with fear as mostly girls call the shots. Boys fear rejection like anyone else.'

Me calling the shots? That was a laugh. But boys being nervous too, that was obvious really. I'd never thought about it before. I'd been so caught up in my own ill-ease, I hadn't thought about theirs. Of course boys must feel that way too sometimes.

'For instance,' said Steve, 'you may think a boy doesn't want to know, but he may be too scared to say anything. I know I am sometimes, you know, if I like someone.'

Maybe that's what Scott had been doing just now, I thought. Acting cool. Afraid I'd reject him. No. Not possible. Or was it? I felt more confused than ever.

'In fact . . .' said Steve.

'How does anyone ever get together then?' I interrupted. 'I think I'd need someone to make it *very* clear to me.'

'How?'

'Dunno. Cards. Presents. Billboard in Piccadilly? Shout from the top of the rooftops I FANCY TJ WATTS.'

Steve laughed. 'I'm sure there are loads of boys after you,' he said. 'You just don't know it.'

'Really?'

'Well you saw the reaction you were getting yesterday.'

'Yeah. But I wasn't sure if that girlie girl look was really my style.'

Steve nodded. 'Yeah. Don't get me wrong, but I thought Nesta had made you into a Nesta clone. That look suits her, but I see you more as Buffy than Barbie.'

'Really?' Cool, I thought. I liked the sound of that. More Buffy than Barbie. I must make a note of what kind of clothes she wears.

'So how's the mag going?'

'OK. But it's brought out the competitive side of everyone at school. And some of them can be pretty bitchy. Like there's this one girl, the one we saw in Hampstead. She's giving me a really hard time.' I continued filling him in on the Dog of the Week stunt that Wendy had pulled. 'Wendy Roberts.'

Steve slapped his forehead. 'The one outside Accessorize? I *knew* I knew her. Now you say the name . . . A mate of mine went out with her.' Then he chuckled. 'I could tell you some good goss about her.'

'What?'

'No front teeth.'

'How do you know?'

'My mate found out when he snogged her. One of them came loose. That's how I remember her name. She's waiting for implants but the dentist won't do them until she's older. So she's got dentures. Real false teeth. Apparently she knocked both of them out in a riding accident. You could print a piece about dentists. And put in a picture of her as an example.'

I laughed at the thought of it. 'With a caption. All I want for Christmas is my two front teeth.'

'Or instead of wide-eyed and legless, you could write, wide-eyed and toothless.'

'Don't tempt me,' I said.

The time whizzed by as we chatted on about ideas for the school newsletter and Steve offered to do a piece on photography.

When I looked at my watch, it said eight o'clock.

'God, I'd better go,' I said. 'Mum'll kill me.'

We rounded up the dogs, put them back on their leads and Steve walked me to the top of our road.

'So, bye,' he said as we reached our gate.

'Bye.'

He went to go, then turned back.

'Er. Um. Do you . . . would you like to play tennis one day?'

'Sure,' I said. I'd enjoyed the time we spent together and was beginning to think we could be good mates. 'If you're prepared to be beaten.'

email: Outbox (2)
From: goody2shoes@psnet.co.uk
To: paulwatts@worldnet.com
Date: 25 June
Subject: runs

Dear Bro

Sorry to hear about the amoebic dysentery. Have asked
Mum to get you another passport and get it sent to you.
Haven't told Dad. Be careful.

Love

TJ   XXXXXXXXXXXXXXXXXXXXXXXXXXXXXXXXXXXXX

From: goody2shoes@psnet.co.uk
To: nestahotbabe@retro.co.uk
Date: 27 June
Subject: movie

Do you fancy the new Julia Roberts movie on Friday? It's on
at the Hollywood Bowl. Lucy and Izzie are up for it. Hope
you can come.

TJ   XXXXXXXXXXXXXXXXXXXXXXXXXXXXXXXXXXXXX

email:	Inbox (1)
From:	nestahotbabe@retro.co.uk
To:	goody2shoes@psnet.co.uk
Date:	27 June
Subject:	movie

Cool. I'll be dere.

More Buffy than Barbie

To do:

1) Watch Buffy videos to note clothes.
2) Return Dress From Hell and swap for something the Buffster would wear.
3) Go to movie wearing new outfit.

It worked.

'TJ, you look wicked,' said Izzie as we walked from the bus stop towards the Hollywood Bowl the following Friday. 'Your hair looks so much better now you leave it loose and I love the combats.'

Lucy looked me up and down and nodded her approval. 'Yeah. And I'm glad to see you haven't ruined the effect by hiding in a big baggy fleece. The tank top is great.'

'Yeah. Bootylicious,' said Nesta.

I *think* that means she approves.

We made our way through the car park to the cinema and it felt great. I could see groups of lads ogling us. And not just Nesta this time, even I was getting a few looks.

When we got to the foyer, Izzie and Lucy went off to get the tickets while Nesta and I went upstairs and queued up for popcorn. As we were standing in line, I noticed Scott standing at the top of the escalator on his own. He kept checking his watch and looking down towards the entrance as if he was waiting for someone.

After we'd got our popcorn, Scott was still standing on his own, so we found Lucy and Izzie then made our way over to him.

'Been stood up?' asked Nesta.

Lucy punched her arm. '*Nesta!*'

'What?' said Nesta. *'What?'*

'Actually,' said Scott, his face brightening immediately. 'I was waiting for you.'

'As *if*,' said Nesta, tossing her hair.

Scott checked downstairs then, seeing no one was coming up, he linked his arm through hers. 'Looks like my mate has been held up, so the honour of keeping me company is yours.'

'Mate or *date* been held up?' asked Nesta. 'Admit it. You've been stood up.'

Lucy punched her arm again. 'Excuse my *rude* friend,' she said to Scott. 'We don't often let her out at night.'

Scott grinned. 'So, you coming then?' he said to Nesta before turning to the rest of us. 'Sorry, girls. Only got dosh for two tickets.'

Nesta took his arm out of hers and came to stand behind us.

'Actually,' she said. 'I already have plans. With people who actually bother to turn up. Come on, girls. I'm going to the ladies'.'

Scott looked taken aback as we walked off leaving him standing there. As I looked over my shoulder, I couldn't help but feel sorry for him. I know him well enough to recognise that what we'd just witnessed was a huge act of bravado. Everything Steve said to me yesterday came flooding back. How hard it is for boys to take rejection even if they don't show it. It still hurts. His date hadn't shown and Nesta had made a fool of him on top of everything else.

As we stood in front of the mirrors doing our hair and lippie and stuff, I made up my mind.

'I'm going to ask if Scott would like me to go with him to a movie.'

'No,' chorused Izzie, Lucy and Nesta.

'Why not? He's been let down. He probably feels lousy.'

'Who? Scott? Nah, he's well sure of himself,' said Nesta. 'He thinks he's God's gift and could probably do with being brought down a peg or two.'

'No, he's really sweet underneath. It's all an act,' I said.

'Ah,' sighed Lucy. 'Love is blind.'

'Well, you don't want to be too easy if you really like him,' said Iz. 'You need to play hard to get. Boys like the chase.'

'But I feel sorry for him,' I said. 'I'm going to go and ask him.'

'How can someone with so many brains be so stupid?' asked Nesta as Lucy sighed in exasperation.

'You can think what you like,' I said, as I did a last check of my appearance. 'But I've known him longer than you and this is something I have to do.'

With that, I turned on my heel. As the loo door closed behind me, I could hear Lucy telling Nesta off for being insensitive.

'Yeah. OK, then,' said Scott, when I told him that I'd keep him company. 'But I'm not going to see the same movie as your mates.'

'But Izzie already got me a ticket.'

'I'm not sitting anywhere near that lesbian.'

'Lesbian?'

'Nesta.'

I laughed. Sour grapes, I thought, but I didn't say anything. He was just lashing out because she'd humiliated him in front of the rest of us.

There were five other films on at the complex so I let him pick what we were going to see. He chose a sci-fi film.

'I'm not mad on sci-fi,' I said. 'Are you sure you don't want to see the new comedy with Julia Roberts? I've heard it's a real laugh. And we can sit on the other side from the girls.'

'No way,' said Scott. 'The sci-fi or I'm going home.'

In the end, I gave in. I didn't mind. What I really wanted was a chance to spend some time with Scott alone and see what happened.

Scott loved the film, but I couldn't concentrate. As the screen filled with manic scenes from intergalactic wars, I was only aware of the proximity of Scott. Our knees and elbows touched a couple of times and I was hoping that he would hold my hand, but he just stuffed his face with popcorn.

Maybe real life isn't like the movies, I thought, as another alien got his three heads ripped off, squirting green blood all over the hero. Maybe in real life, romance isn't beautiful sunsets and gentle kisses. Maybe in real life, romance is sitting in the dark wondering if the boy you're with is *ever* going to make a move that isn't him merely shifting position in his seat. Maybe romance is all fantasy. For the last few days, that's all I'd done. Every night before I went to sleep, I imagined my first kiss with Scott. First he'd push a lock of hair behind my ear, then look deeply into my eyes, then softly press his lips on mine and . . .

A *phwt* noise beside me disturbed my thoughts.

Scott had farted.

'Oops,' he said with a grin. 'Popcorn-flavoured.'

★ ★ ★

After the movie, we made our way out back into the foyer and Scott was a few steps in front of me. Suddenly, he spotted a few of his mates who had been with him in Hampstead on the day of the photo shoot.

One of them came over.

'You're the girl who was having her photo taken the other day, aren't you?' he asked.

I nodded.

'You looked really good,' he said.

'Thanks.'

Suddenly, Scott took my hand.

'Yeah, this is TJ,' he said, as he introduced the group of boys.

Then he put his arm round me. 'Just been to see *Alien Mutants in Cyberspace*,' he said, then winked at them. 'Didn't get to see much of the film, though, if ya know what I mean . . .'

The boys sniggered knowingly.

'Anyway, got to go,' said Scott and looked at me fondly. 'The night is young.'

'Yeah, right,' said one of the boys as Scott pulled me away.

What was going on? I wondered. Did he fancy me after all and, as Steve said, had been acting cool? Or was this all a big act to make his mates think we were on a date? He still had hold of my hand as we went down the escalator and out the foyer but, unlike the day in Hampstead, I wasn't feeling all fluttery inside. I felt muddled. I didn't want to take my hand away though, as I remembered what he'd said about the night being young. Things could only get better.

When we got outside, I suggested we go and have a cappuccino.

'Got no money left,' he said.

'No prob. My treat.'

Scott shrugged. 'OK, then. And a hot dog?'

'Fine,' I said.

'With onions.'

'Fine.'

For the next half hour, he talked. I listened.

He talked.

He talked.

I listened.

I was bursting to tell him all about my last few weeks. Emails from Hannah and Paul. The magazine. My new mates. So much had happened, but I couldn't get a word in edgeways. He talked, I listened. That was the deal and always has been since I'd known him. I'd just never been bothered about it before. As I tried to appear interested, I thought that even Mojo was more interested in what I had to say. And he's a dog.

'So, enough about me. What about you?' he said, finally pausing for breath. 'What do you think of me?'

Then he laughed like he'd said the funniest thing ever.

I couldn't help but think how easy Steve had been to

talk to. We'd never shut up the other day in the park. But with him, it had been equal. I talked, he listened. He talked, I listened. He'd seemed interested in what I had to say and what my opinions were.

I took a long look at Scott. No doubt he was mucho cute to look at. A lovely curly mouth and deep-brown eyes. But as I stared into them, I thought, Scott Harris, I've never realised this before but you are boring. As in B. O. R. *iiing*.

I had a sudden urge to go home, talk to Mojo, email Hannah and even maybe catch up with Steve. He had promised to start work on his article for the magazine and I could call to see how it was coming along.

We got the bus home together and when we got to our houses, Scott did a quick check up and down the street, then up at the windows. I was about to go in, when he suddenly pushed me against the wall and the next thing I knew I was being snogged.

My first snog.

Ugh. Agh, I thought as his mouth crashed into mine. And erlack, onions. His mouth tasted ukky. It was a really wet, slimy kiss, not how I'd imagined it at all.

When he'd finished cleaning my teeth with his tongue, he stood back, looking really pleased with himself.

'Catcha later,' he said, pointing his index finger at me. Then he turned and went inside.

'Not if I see you first,' I thought as I wiped my mouth on my arm.

★ ★ ★

A couple of hours later, I was up in my room working on some ideas for the magazine when the phone went.

'TJ, it's Nesta.'

'Oh, hi . . . Nes . . .'

'Listen,' interrupted Nesta. 'I've got something to say to you and I hope you won't take it the wrong way, but, well, that boy Scott . . . he's not the one for you. Don't ask me how I know, I just do. He thinks too much of himself and I know boys like that look pretty, but all they are interested in is themselves. You deserve better. You mustn't be a doormat. You can do better, believe me. It's just you're suffering from low self-esteem, but someone will come along who you'll have a better time with. Who really wants to be with you. Because you are a babe. With brains. Lethal combination as I've said before. And I know you like Scott and now you're probably going to hate me and not speak to me, but as a friend I felt I had to tell you. TJ, are you there? Do you hate me now? Please say something? Oh, hell bells and poo. Lucy said I shouldn't phone but Izzie said I should. TJ, TJ . . .?'

I couldn't say anything because I was too busy laughing and I'd put my hand over the phone so she couldn't hear.

'Nesta. I agree.'

'You . . . you *what?*'

'Yeah, you're right. Scott Harris. Cute but dull. Dull as dishwater. And . . . he's a bad snogger.'

'He *snogged* you!' exclaimed Nesta. '*Ohmigod*. Details.'

We spent the next half-hour yabbering about snogs

and Nesta told me all about some of her early disasters.

'It's not always like that,' she said in the end.

'Phewww,' I said. 'So there's hope.'

'Mucho mucho,' said Nesta. 'It can be just how you imagined it and better.'

When I put down the phone, I felt really happy. That night, as I fell asleep, a different boy seemed to have taken Scott's place in my snogging fantasy.

email:	Outbox (1)
From:	babewithbrains@psnet.co.uk
To:	nestahotbabe@retro.co.uk
Date:	29 June
Subject:	new email

Note new email address. Whatdoyathink?

TJ

email: Inbox (2)
From: nestahotbabe@retro.co.uk
To: babewithbrains@psnet.co.uk
Date: 29 June
Subject: new email

Bootylicious. See you tomorrow pm at Lucy's for the magazine finale.

   Nesta

From: paulwatts@worldnet.com
To: babewithbrains@psnet.co.uk
Date: 29 June
Subject: hol

Hi TJ

Holiday really not going as planned. Monsoons have hit the resort. Torrential rain so impossible to sleep on beach. Am crashing in a hut with four other travellers, but caught head lice after I borrowed a sleeping bag (mine was nicked), Oh, and to top it all, Saskia has run away with the holy man from Kilburn. I have the runs and mosquito bites as big as golf balls.

   Hope all well your end.
   Love

   Paul

PS Please ask Dad to send very strong medical supplies. Anything and everything.

Chapter 13

The Mad House

The next afternoon, I had half of North London employed as my editorial staff.

At home, I'd asked Mum and Dad each to write something.

'We're theming the magazine towards summer,' I said to Dad, 'so I'd like you to do some handy hints for travelling abroad from a doctor's point of view. Make it relevant. A mini medical cabinet that you could pack in a suitcase. Stuff for sunburn, mosquitoes, the runs and so on.'

'Will do,' he said with a grin.

I think he was really chuffed to have been asked.

And Mum was doing an article on how to deal with exam stress.

'Ten handy hints,' I said. 'It has to be accessible.'

I left them listening to Radio 4 and sipping Earl Grey tea as they worked.

Over at Nesta's, Tony was working on a cartoon for a competition. We were going to invite readers to send in captions and print the best in the next edition. If there *was* a next edition.

At Lucy's, Steve and I worked on the computer in his and Lal's bedroom.

Lucy and Nesta were finishing their articles in the living-room.

Izzie was on the computer in Lucy's bedroom, working out horoscopes for the coming month.

Mrs Lovering kept bringing us herbie drinks with ginseng and some icky-tasting stuff called Guryana.

'Keeps you alert,' she said.

And Mr Lovering sat in the kitchen playing his guitar.

'Music to inspire the workers,' he said, when I went down to ask for a new ink cartridge for the printer. How a rendition of You Ain't Nothing But a Hound Dog was supposed to motivate us, I have no idea, but Ben and Jerry seemed to like it as they joined in, howling away with great gusto.

'This place is a *mad* house,' said Lal, looking at his dad with disapproval. 'I'm off somewhere normal. Where I can *think* in peace!'

'Go to my house, then,' I said. 'It's like a morgue.'

No one's ever happy with their lot, I thought, as I watched him storm off in a huff. I'm sure Mum and Dad would agree with Lal if they came over but I loved it. Mr L (as Izzie calls him) is a real laugh and as opposite to my dad as anyone you could meet. He's an old hippie who's losing his hair, yet has a ponytail. And he wears very bright Hawaiian shirts and Indian sandals. Mrs L is hippie-dippie too, today wearing a Peruvian skirt with mirrors round the hem and a rather strange crocheted top.

'You OK, TJ?' asked Steve, when I went back upstairs. 'You're kind of quiet today.'

'Yuh, yunewee,' I muttered.

A *lot* had happened in the last twenty-four hours. Mainly in my head. I'd had my eyes opened to what a user Scott was and I was experiencing an almighty twinge of conscience that I'd treated Steve the same way. Someone to earbash with my problems. Only last week I'd been on about how much I fancied Scott and how he never noticed me and treated me like a mate and nothing more. That was *exactly* how I'd treated Steve. And he'd been so sweet, reassuring me that I was fanciable and telling me how boys really felt about girls.

As I sat next to him at the desk, I felt the warmth of his arm against mine and caught the scent of soap on his skin. Back came the old fluttery feeling, only this time, I was with Steve, not Scott. How had I not noticed what nice eyes he had? Kind. Hazel-brown with honey flecks around the iris. And good hands, I thought, as he pressed keys on the computer keyboard, long fingers, elegant.

And it was too late. If I said anything, he'd think I was a complete airhead. Fickle and a half. In love with Scott one week, fancying him the next.

'So have you decided what to do about Wendy Roberts and her dentures?' asked Steve, leaning over me to see what I'd written.

'Er, *yu . . . nu . . . wee . . .* Wendy, yes. I've decided I'm not going to stoop to her level. I'll save stuff like that for my secret notebook and use it later when I write novels.'

'Good for you,' said Steve. 'So do you reckon we'll be ready to hand the mag in on Monday?'

'*Nih . . . ing . . . yah . . .*' I said, cursing Alien Girl who had taken over my vocal chords. 'Umost. I mean, almost.'

Steve was looking at me as though I had two heads.

'Gottask Luceand Nestasomething. Backinaminute,' I said, jumping up.

I stumbled downstairs to find Lucy and Nesta. I needed help.

I sat on the floor and put my head in my hands. 'Ag. Agh. Agherama.'

'Hey, it'll be all right. We're almost there,' said Nesta. 'We'll do it on time.'

'Do what?' I said, looking up.

'The mag.'

'Oh it's not that. It's . . .' I looked at Lucy. Steve was her brother. What would *she* think if she knew I'd been fantasising about him? She knew how I felt about Scott. She'd think I was a complete tart for changing my mind so fast.

'So what is it?' asked Lucy.

'Nothing,' I said.

'Yeah, looks like it,' said Nesta. 'Come on, spill.'

I sighed. Then looked at the two of them waiting expectantly. Then I sighed again.

Nesta and Lucy started doing big sighs as well. Then really exaggerating them, heaving huge extended breaths until I had to laugh.

'OK. Lie out on the sofa,' said Lucy.

I did as I was told and Lucy sat at the other end.

'So Miss Vatts. Vat seems to be ze problem?'

I couldn't say. Silence. Big silence. It grew and filled the room.

'Ah. Boy trouble,' said Lucy.

'But which boy?' said Nesta. 'You're over Scott *n'est-ce pas?*'

I nodded. 'It's another boy who I've only just realised I like. Much nicer than Scott. And now I'm all tongue-tied and stupid around him. And I think I've blown it. And it's probably too late.'

'Oh, you mean *Steve?*' asked Lucy.

'*How* did you know?'

'Kind of obvious from the start,' said Lucy.

'*Obvious?* To *who*? *I've* only just realised. And who knows what's going on in his head. If he likes *me.*'

'Er, *hello?*' said Lucy. 'What planet are you on exactly?'

'Planet Zog, actually,' I said and explained all about Noola and her ability to take over my head.

'Well, for your information, Steve hasn't stopped talking about you and asking about you ever since he met you,' said Lucy. 'And he was well miffed with the fact you fancied Scott. Didn't you notice how weirded out he was when we bumped into Scott in Hampstead?'

'Suppose he was kind of quiet that day. I thought I'd done something to upset him.'

'D'oh. *Yeah*. You had,' said Lucy. 'Fancied someone else.'

Izzie came down the stairs and flopped on the sofa.

'Whassup?' she asked.

'TJ,' said Nesta. 'She turns into Noola the Alien Girl whenever she fancies a boy. Noola only knows three words. Tell her, TJ.'

'*Uhyuh. Yunewee*. And *nihingyah*.'

Lucy started giggling and doing an alien robot impersonation like CP30 in *Star Wars* up and down the room.

'*Uhyuh*,' she squeaked in a high voice. '*Yunewee. Nihingyaaaah*.'

We were laughing so hard that Steve came down to see what was going on. Of course, I went purple.

'So?' said Steve.

'So noth . . . nothing,' chuckled Nesta.

'Just something Lucy said,' said Izzie.

Steve looked up to the heavens, then turned to me. 'You coming back to finish your editorial?'

'Uh . . . *uhyuh*,' I said and Lucy exploded with laughter.

Steve heaved a sigh, which Lucy and Nesta copied.

Steve looked at us all as though we were stupid. '*When* you're ready, TJ,' he said and went back to his room.

'See, do you *see* now?' I said. 'I'm going to blow it. And we were getting on so well and now I'm going to act like an idiot around him and he'll think I'm Dork from Dorkland, Nerd from Nerdville, Airhead from . . .'

'Shut the door, Lucy,' said Izzie. 'We clearly have work to do.'

We spent the next twenty minutes doing a visualisation with Izzie. She's well into self-help stuff and had been reading in one of her books about positive thinking.

'It's all in the mind,' she said. 'You can get over this and put Noola the Alien Girl to rest. But you have to see yourself acting confidently. I've been reading all about it for when I do gigs.'

'But I think you're either confident or not,' I said. 'Like Nesta. It's not something you can learn.'

'Oh, yes it is,' said Nesta. 'We all have our own tricks. Sometimes, I pretend I'm a character out of a film if I feel nervous. Then I act as I think they would. It really works.'

'And I used to be hopeless about singing in public,' said Izzie. 'So bad I couldn't sleep at night. I used to be well terrified of looking a fool and this has really helped.'

'So, you think I could learn to talk sense when I meet a boy I like?'

'Definitely,' said Izzie. 'In fact, my book says, "we are what we repeatedly do. Confidence is not an act but a habit." You have to practise.'

'Cool,' said Lucy. 'Sounds good to me. What do we do?'

Izzie made us all sit down and close our eyes. First, we had to imagine the situation we felt nervous in, so I thought about being close to Steve upstairs. We had to imagine the room, the surroundings, what we were wearing, all the details.

Then Izzie said, 'Imagine yourself being relaxed, calm and completely in control. Imagine the other person's response to you. In your mind, see them laughing at your jokes, listening with interest to what you say, *liking* you.'

She made us imagine the situation over and over again until in my imagination, Steve was gawping at me in open admiration, amazed at my witticisms. In *awe* at my brilliant conversation.

'OK, open your eyes, everyone.'

We did as we were told and looked around at each other.

'How do you feel now, TJ?'

I stood up and went to the door. 'Awesome. Noola. She dead.' I put my hands on my hips Arnold Schwarzeneggar style and said, 'I'll be back. Hasta la vista, baby.'

Nesta laughed. 'Go get him, girlfriend.'

I went back up the stairs. As I stood outside Steve's bedroom, my butterfly nerves came back, so I imagined Steve smiling at me and enjoying my company.

I went in, sat down next to him at the computer, did a quick visualisation in my head, then turned and gave him a huge smile.

He turned to look at me. 'Aaagjjhh. What's the matter with you *now*?'

'Nothing,' I beamed, thinking, I am confident, I am great, stunning, brill, dazzling, fantabulous.

Steve looked at me as though I was totally bonkers.

'You're *really* weird, you know that, don't you?' he asked.

Just at that moment, my mobile went.

'Scuse, Steve,' I said, as I put the phone to my ear.

'Hey, TJ,' said Scott's voice. 'What you doing?'

'Magazine. Remember, I told you. Deadline Monday.'

'Oh, that can wait,' said Scott. 'Wanna go out to the Heath?'

'Sorry, Scott,' I said. 'Busy. Later.'

Then I hung up.

'That guy?' asked Steve.

'That guy.'

'And . . .?'

'And . . . history,' I said.

Now Steve had a huge grin across his face.

'What's the matter?' I asked.

'Nothing,' he beamed.

'You're *really* weird,' I said. 'You know that, don't you?'

'Yeah,' he nodded. 'So that makes two of us.'

For Real

Summer edition

Contents

Chapter 14

Sabotage

The magazine looked great. We'd done the final layout on Steve's computer, eight full pages that looked fun and interesting.

Steve had found all sorts of visuals on the Internet to liven up the articles, pictures of dogs for the Battersea Dogs' Home article, stars for the horoscope page, herbs and flowers for Izzie's aromatherapy piece. Plus the mad 'before' and 'after' make-over photographs for the centre spread.

It looked good. Very good. I reckoned I was in with a chance.

At assembly on Monday, Mrs Allen asked that all entries were handed in to our form teacher.

'I know a lot of you have worked very hard on this,' she said, 'so we won't keep you waiting. We hope to have an announcement about the winner by the end of the week.'

Five minutes later, we filed into class and I joined the group hovering around Miss Watkins' desk. I put my copy on the small pile of entries from our class.

'Quite a number getting it all finished on time, wasn't it?' I asked Wendy Roberts who was standing behind me.

'Er, *no*,' she said. 'Unlike some saddos in this class, I didn't do one. See, I have a life.'

'Oh, I thought you were into it.'

'You thought wrong. Deadlines are for losers. And, by the way, Mrs Allen said she wanted to see you. I saw her just now in the corridor. She wanted you to go to her office immediately.'

That's strange, I thought, as I hurried off down the corridor to Mrs Allen's office. I hoped nothing was wrong.

'Mrs Allen wants to see me,' I said as her secretary looked up when I knocked on the office door.

'I don't think so, dear,' she said. 'Mrs Allen's in with Mr Parker. She said not to be disturbed. Must be some mistake.'

No mistake, I thought, as I went back to class. I suppose Wendy thought she was being funny.

Miss Watkins was at her desk flicking through the entries when I walked back into the class. 'You're late, TJ,' she said.

'Er, sorry, miss,' I said, going to my desk.

Luckily, she didn't go on about it, as Wendy Roberts came in just behind me.

'And you, Roberts, what's your excuse?'

'Loo, miss,' she said, breathlessly taking her place.

Miss Watkins continued flicking through the entries. 'Well done girls, we have six entries from this class.' Then she looked at me. 'But I thought we'd have had one more. I thought you were going to enter, TJ.'

'I *did*, Miss,' I said. 'I put it in the pile after assembly.'

'Well, it's not here now,' she said.

I looked round at Wendy Roberts. She was gazing out of the window, looking like butter wouldn't melt in her mouth.

'Are you sure, TJ?' said Miss Watkins. 'Check your bag.'

I did as I was told, but I was sure I'd put it on the desk. 'Not there, miss.'

'So where is it?'

Suddenly, I didn't know what to say. And I had no proof that Wendy had taken it.

'Maybe it's fallen on the floor?'

Miss Watkins had a quick look around, then faced the class.

'Has anyone taken TJ's entry?'

No one spoke.

'This is very serious. If TJ says she put her entry on the pile then either she's lying or someone's taken it. Is anyone going to enlighten me?'

Again no one spoke.

'She *did* do an entry,' said Lucy. 'I saw it. Honest, miss.'

Miss Watkins looked upset. 'This is *very* unfortunate, girls. It's almost the end of term and next year, you'll be going into Year 10. You're not beginners any more and, frankly, I'm disappointed in this sort of behaviour. However, I'm going to ask you to act like mature adults and sort this out amongst yourselves. Twelve-thirty this lunch-time is the deadline for entries, so unless you find it, TJ, or someone owns up, I'm afraid there's not a lot more I'm prepared to do.'

'That cow,' said Lucy, as we filed out at break-time. 'I'm sure it was Wendy Roberts.'

'Did anyone see anything?' I asked.

Nesta shook her head. 'She must have taken it from Miss Watkins' desk when you went to see Mrs Allen.'

'There was a whole crowd round Miss Watkins' desk,' said Izzie. 'Anyone could have taken it. You know how competitive everyone's been.'

'But Wendy did come in after you, TJ. You know, before lessons started. Remember?' said Izzie.

'To the loos,' said Nesta. 'Let's go.'

We ran down the corridor to the cloakrooms. Lucy looked in the cubicles while Nesta searched in the bin.

'Er*lack*,' said Nesta, as she rummaged around amongst bits of old tissue and paper towels.

'Oh, *noooo*,' I heard Lucy say, as she reached the third cubicle.

She came out holding a sopping wet pile of ripped paper. 'I'm *so* sorry, TJ, it was in the bin next to the loo.'

Izzie took what was left of the magazine. 'It looks like she's run it under the tap first.'

'But *why*?' I said. 'Why has she got it in for me?'

'Doesn't have to be a reason,' sighed Nesta. 'Some people are just very *very* sad. They can't stand to see anyone else doing well.'

'I reckon she never got over being made to look an idiot when Sam Denham was here,' said Izzie. 'You know, when he praised your answer and dismissed hers.'

'What are we going to do?' I said, leaning back against one of the sinks. 'I can't hand it in like this.'

'We could go to Mrs Allen,' said Nesta.

I was gutted. 'We could, but what will that achieve? Only make Wendy hate me more. The main thing is, my entry's unreadable. *All* that work, wasted.' I was near to tears. 'And all your contributions.'

Lucy got her mobile out of her bag. 'What time is it?' she said.

'Eleven,' I said.

She began dialling frantically.

'Who are you phoning? I asked.

'Steve,' she said. 'His year's doing exams and stuff so their timetable's all over the place. He might be at home revising.'

'Brill,' said Izzie. 'He's got the mag on his computer. It will only take a minute to print out.'

'That's if he's there,' said Nesta.

Lucy listened as the phone rang, then she grimaced. 'Voicemail,' she said. 'He must be doing something.'

'Leave a message anyway,' said Izzie. 'It's our only chance.'

We went back into the next lesson, but I couldn't concentrate. And neither could Nesta, Izzie or Lucy, by the looks of it.

'If you look at your watch one more time, TJ Watts,' said Mr Dixon, 'I'm going to take it off you. And Lucy Lovering, if whatever you're staring at outside the window is so fascinating, I suggest you go and stand there for the rest of the lesson.'

I glanced across at Wendy Roberts. She looked up from her book and smiled smugly.

You just wait, Wendy Roberts, I thought. It's not over yet.

We flew out of the classroom at lunch-time and out into the playground towards the gates.

No one there.

Lucy got out her phone again. She dialled, then shook her head. 'Still on voicemail.'

I checked my watch. Ten past twelve.

Twelve-fifteen.

Twelve-twenty.

'Did you say what time the deadline was when you left the message?' asked Nesta, looking up and down the street anxiously.

'Yeah,' said Lucy. 'I said twelve-thirty. I'll try ringing again.'

She was about to dial, when Izzie grabbed my arm.

'Here he is,' she cried, as Steve came flying round the corner on his bike.

He screeched to a stop and pulled an envelope out of his rucksack.

'Good luck,' he said, as he handed it over.

'Thanks,' I called over my shoulder as I ran back inside. This time I wasn't taking any chances.

I went straight to the staff room and asked for Miss Watkins. I wanted to put my magazine into her hands myself.

Result

'And the new editor will be . . .' said Mrs Allen, as we stood in assembly on Friday.

I held my breath as Nesta gave me the thumbs-up.

'Before I announce the winner, I must say it's been very difficult,' continued Mrs Allen. 'The standard of entries was exceptionally high and I'm very proud of all of you. Ultimately, there are no losers. We've had a very hard time deciding and . . .'

Izzie gave me a look as if to say, 'I wish she'd get on with it.'

'Finally, we narrowed it down to two. We decided on a tie. Two winners. First, Emma Ford from Year 10. And, second, TJ Watts from Year 9.'

There were cheers from Nesta, Izzie and Lucy at the back of the class. But, best of all, Wendy Roberts' face was a picture. Her mouth literally dropped open.

I gave her a huge smile as I went up to join Emma on the stage with Mrs Allen.

★ ★ ★

After school, we all piled back to Lucy's for celebratory ice cream and cake. When the girls were settled chomping away, Steve beckoned me up to his room.

'I . . . I have something for you,' he said shyly.

He went to a drawer in the cabinet next to his bed. He pulled out a small package wrapped in silver, with a gold bow and a card and handed them to me. 'These are for you.'

I opened the card first. On the front it had a black-and-white photograph of a man on a road, with a caption underneath saying, 'Life shrinks or expands in proportion to one's courage.' Inside he'd written, 'Good Luck to the new Editor of *For Real*.'

'Thanks. That's really . . .'

'Open the pressie,' he said, smiling.

I ripped off the paper and found a beautiful pen inside. It was Indian-looking, shiny turquoise and silver with sequinny things on the side.

'*Yu . . . nu . . . wee*,' I said, slipping back into Zoganese for a moment.

'You're welcome,' he said, as if he understood perfectly. 'It's for writing your novels.'

For a moment, we just stayed looking at each other. It was the most perfect feeling. Like time stopped still and we were somehow melting into each other.

Then Steve grinned. 'So next . . .?'

'Next?' I asked. 'What do you mean? Next?'

'That day in the park, when you asked how does

153

anyone ever get together and you said for you, they'd have to make it *really* obvious – pressies, cards, a billboard in Piccadilly . . .'

I looked at my card and my present and smiled. 'Oh. But please, no, not a billboard in Piccadilly, I'd *die* . . .'

Steve laughed, then leant towards me, pushed a lock of hair away from my face, looked deeply into my eyes and . . .

'We could go and see a movie next,' he said.

'Love to,' I said. 'As long as it's not *Alien Mutants in Cyberspace*. And you don't spend the whole movie eating popcorn.'

'Deal. Anyway, I hate popcorn.'

We sort of grinned stupidly at each other, then I remembered what he'd said that day in the park. That he sometimes felt scared when he liked a girl.

No time like the present, I thought, as I leaned in and kissed him softly on the lips.

email:	Inbox (1)
From:	paulwatts@worldnet.com
To:	babewithbrains@psnet.co.uk
Date:	5 July
Subject:	hol

Dear TJ

New passport received this morning.
   Coming home.

   Paul

email: Outbox (1)
To: hannahnutter@fastmail.com
From: babewithbrains@psnet.co.uk
Date: 5 July
Subject: mates, dates

Hey Hannahnutter

Whassup? Sorry I haven't been in touch, it's been mad here. So much has been happening. Paul's coming home. Scott is history. Got a date with Steve. Realised boys can be mates as well as dates. Der. Took me a while!

Velly happy. Hope you are.

And I won the competition with Emma Ford from Year 10. I am now the new joint-editor of the school magazine. Hurrah.

TJ XXXXXXXXXXXXXXXXXXXXXXXXXXXXXXXXXXXXXXX

```
email:      Inbox (1)
From:       hannahnutter@fastmail.com
To:         babewithbrains@psnet.co.uk
Date:       5 July
Subject:    Goody flobbalots
```

Velly solly me no been in touch either.

Goody flobbalots and hurrah about mag thing. I knew you'd get it.

And coolerooney about Steve. I could tell even from a zillion trillion miles away that something was going to 'appen zere. Hasta la banana and many jolly jollities to him. He soundeth superbio. A mate and a date. Best kind.

Mad here too. Replaced ze Luke with ze Ryan. So many boys, so little time etc etc. Most excellent fun here. Loadsa big bashes and barbies, though I truly miss you and your strange angle on life and SOH.

Send me photos of your new look. And new boy. And new mag.

At last le TJ has recognised she is ze babe *avec* ze brain.

Keep buzy and yabberyabber spoon.

Lurve and keesses

Your friend for ever and ever and ever and ever and ever and ever and . . . (oh, shutup H)

www.piccadillypress.co.uk

☆ The latest news on forthcoming books

☆ Chapter previews

☆ Author biographies

☆ Fun quizzes

☆ Reader reviews

☆ Competitions and fab prizes

☆ Book features and cool downloads

☆ And much, much more . . .

Log on and check it out!

Piccadilly Press

100

words every high school graduate should **know**

THE **100 WORDS**® *From the Editors of the*
AMERICAN HERITAGE®
DICTIONARIES

HOUGHTON MIFFLIN
Boston   New York

EDITORIAL STAFF OF THE

American Heritage® Dictionaries

MARGERY S. BERUBE, *Vice President, Publisher of Dictionaries*

JOSEPH P. PICKETT, *Vice President, Executive Editor*

DAVID R. PRITCHARD, *Editorial Project Director*

STEVEN R. KLEINEDLER, *Senior Editor*

BENJAMIN W. FORTSON, IV, *Senior Lexicographer*

HANNA SCHONTHAL, *Editor*

VALI TAMM, *Editor*

MATTHEW HEIDENRY, *Associate Editor*

KIRSTEN PATEY, *Associate Editor*

UCHENNA C. IKONNÉ, *Assistant Editor*

THE 100 WORDS® is a registered trademark of Houghton Mifflin Company.

American Heritage and the eagle logo are registered trademarks of American Heritage Inc. Their use is pursuant to a license agreement with American Heritage Inc.

Visit our websites: www.ahdictionary.com
or www.houghtonmifflinbooks.com

LIBRARY OF CONGRESS CATALOGING-IN-PUBLICATION DATA

100 words every high school graduate should know / from the editors of the American heritage dictionaries.
p. cm.
Based on the 4th ed. of the American Heritage college dictionary.
ISBN 0-618-37412-4
1. Vocabulary. I. Title: One hundred words every high school graduate should know. II. American Heritage college dictionary.
PE1449.A145   2003   428.1--dc21   2003040668

Text design by Anne Chalmers

MANUFACTURED IN THE UNITED STATES OF AMERICA

EB 20 19 18 17 16 15

Table of Contents

℘

One Hundred Words
Every High School Graduate
Should Know

Preface

The editors of the *American Heritage College Dictionary, Fourth Edition,* originally developed the *100 Words Every High School Graduate Should Know* to highlight the importance of owning and using a dictionary. We provided journalists and radio announcers across the United States with this list, and it quickly became the topic of many articles and broadcasts. The list was a hit, and the phenomenal response from the public pleasantly surprised us. Visitors to our website, www.ahdictionary.com, viewed this list over 200,000 times. We were also often asked if the list was available in book form, and this book was published in response to those requests.

The editorial staff found the development of the list to be an engaging and entertaining task. In addition to carefully choosing a well-balanced mix of terms from A to Z, we balanced straightforward vocabulary entries, such as *bellicose, loquacious,* and *vehement,* with words chosen directly from the disciplines of learning, such as *parabola* and *hypotenuse* from mathematics, *gerrymander* and *enfranchise* from civics, and *photosynthesis* and *hemoglobin* from biology. As a result, students often have an easier time with the list than adults, especially if they've been paying attention in their classes!

Still, we intentionally crafted this list to present a challenge to students and adults. Reporters and commentators, especially those who are also parents, have been pleased to find a way to get children and teenagers interested in building a more sophisticated vocabulary —while finding themselves learning as well. We have been delighted by the positive response, and we are

encouraged by the fact that people are taking a closer look at literacy and vocabulary building as an integral part of using dictionaries. We've set the bar high, and people are responding enthusiastically to the challenge.

The following entries are based on material from our *American Heritage Dictionary* series and are presented in an expanded layout that is easy to read. We've added quotations and example sentences to provide greater context for many definitions. To encourage study skills, at the end of this book we have provided exercises for improving vocabulary and encouraging active use of the dictionary.

We hope that you find learning these words and expanding your vocabulary to be a rewarding experience.

Steve Kleinedler,
Senior Editor

Guide to the Entries

ENTRY WORD The 100 words that constitute this book are listed alphabetically. The entry words, along with inflected and derived forms, are divided into syllables by centered dots. These dots show you where you would break the word at the end of a line. The pronunciation of the word follows the entry word. Please see the pronunciation guide and key on pages x–xi for an explanation of the pronunciation system.

PART OF SPEECH At least one part of speech follows each entry word. The part of speech tells you the grammatical category that the word belongs to. Parts of speech include *noun, adjective, adverb, transitive verb,* and *intransitive verb.* (A transitive verb is a verb that needs an object to complete its meaning. *Wash* is transitive in the sentence *I washed the car.* The direct object of *wash* is *the car.* An intransitive verb is one that does not take an object, as *sleep* in the sentence *I slept for seven hours.* Many verbs are both transitive and intransitive.)

INFLECTIONS A word's inflected form differs from the main entry form by the addition of a suffix or by a change in its base form to indicate grammatical features such as number, person, or tense. They are set in boldface type, divided into syllables, and given pronunciations as necessary. The past tense, past participle, and the third person singular present tense inflections of all verbs are shown. The plurals of nouns are shown when they are spelled in a way other than by adding *s* to the base form.

LABELS A subject label identifies the special area of knowledge a definition applies to, as at **metamorphosis.** Information applicable only to a particular sense is shown after the number or letter of that sense; at **metamorphosis,** the biology sense is applicable to sense 2.

The *Usage Problem* label warns of possible difficulties involving grammar, diction, and writing style. A word or definition with this label is discussed in a Usage Note, as at **paradigm.**

Certain nouns are spelled as plurals but sometimes take a singular verb. This information is indicated in italic type, as at **thermodynamics.**

ORDER OF SENSES Entries having more than one sense are arranged with the central and often the most commonly sought meaning first. Senses and subsenses are grouped to show their relationships with each other. Boldface letters before senses indicate that two or more subsenses are closely related, as at **parameter.**

In an entry with more than one part of speech, the senses are numbered in separate sequences after each part of speech, as at **kowtow**.

EXAMPLES OF USAGE Examples often follow the definitions and are set in italic type. These examples show the entry words in typical contexts. Sometimes the examples are quotations from authors of books or newspaper articles. These quotations are shown within quotation marks and are followed by the quotation's author and source.

ETYMOLOGIES Etymologies appear in square brackets following the last definition. An etymology traces the history of a word as far back in time as can be determined with reasonable certainty. The stage most closely preceding Modern English is given first, with each earlier stage following in sequence. A language name, linguistic form (in italics), and brief definition of the form are given for each stage of the derivation. To avoid redundancy, a language, form, or definition is not repeated if it is identical to the corresponding item in the immediately preceding stage. Occasionally, a form will be given that is not actually preserved in written documents but which scholars are confident did exist—such a form will be marked by an asterisk (*). The word *from* is used to indicate origin of any kind: by inheritance, borrowing, or derivation. When an etymology splits a compound word into parts, a colon introduces the parts and each element is then traced back to its origin, with those elements enclosed in parentheses.

RELATED WORDS At the end of many entries, additional boldface words appear without definitions. These words are related in basic meaning to the entry word and are usually formed from the entry word by the addition of suffixes.

NOTES Some entries include Usage Notes or Word Histories. Usage Notes present important information and guidance on matters of grammar, diction, pronunciation, and nuances. Some refer to responses from our Usage Panel, a group of more than 200 respected writers, scholars, and critics. The editors of the *American Heritage Dictionaries* regularly survey these people on a broad range of usage questions. Word Histories are found at words whose etymologies are of particular interest. The bare facts of the etymology are explained to give a fuller understanding of how important linguistic processes operate, how words move from one language to another, and how the history of an individual word can be related to historical and cultural developments.

The final section of this book contains exercises that are designed to help you further strengthen your vocabulary.

Pronunciation Guide

Pronunciations appear in parentheses after boldface entry words. If a word has more than one pronunciation, the first pronunciation is usually more common than the other, but often they are equally common. Pronunciations are shown after inflections and related words where necessary.

Stress is the relative degree of emphasis that a word's syllables are spoken with. An unmarked syllable has the weakest stress in the word. The strongest, or primary, stress is indicated with a bold mark (ˈ). A lighter mark (ʹ) indicates a secondary level of stress. The stress mark follows the syllable it applies to. Words of one syllable have no stress mark because there is no other stress level that the syllable is compared to.

The key on page xi shows the pronunciation symbols used in this Dictionary. To the right of the symbols are words that show how the symbols are pronounced. The letters whose sound corresponds to the symbols are shown in boldface.

The symbol (ə) is called *schwa*. It represents a vowel with the weakest level of stress in a word. The schwa sound varies slightly according to the vowel it represents or the sounds around it:

a·bun·dant (ə-bŭnʹdənt)   **mo·ment** (mōʹmənt)
civ·il (sĭvʹəl)   **grate·ful** (grātʹfəl)

PRONUNCIATION KEY			
Symbol	**Examples**	**Symbol**	**Examples**
ă	pat	oi	noise
ā	pay	ŏŏ	took
âr	care	ŏŏr	lure
ä	father	ōō	boot
b	bib	ou	out
ch	church	p	pop
d	deed, milled	r	roar
ě	pet	s	sauce
ē	bee	sh	ship, dish
f	fife, phase, rough	t	tight, stopped
g	gag	th	thin
h	hat	*th*	this
hw	which	ŭ	cut
ĭ	pit	ûr	urge, term, firm, word, heard
ī	pie, by		
îr	deer, pier	v	valve
j	judge	w	with
k	kick, cat, pique	y	yes
l	lid, needle	z	zebra, xylem
m	mum	zh	vision, pleasure, garage
n	no, sudden		
ng	thing		
ŏ	pot	ə	about, item, edible, gallop, circus
ō	toe		
ô	caught, paw		
ôr	core	ər	butter

"The strong-bas'd promontory
Have I made shake, and by the spurs pluck'd up
The pine and cedar; graves at my command
Have wak'd their sleepers, op'd, and let 'em forth,
By my so potent art. But this rough magic
I here **abjure**."

—William Shakespeare,
The Tempest

1

ab·jure (ăb-jŏŏr′)

transitive verb

    Past participle and past tense: **ab·jured**
    Present participle: **ab·jur·ing**
    Third person singular present tense: **ab·jures**

1. To recant solemnly; renounce or repudiate: *"But this rough magic I here abjure"* (William Shakespeare, *The Tempest*). **2.** To renounce under oath; forswear: *The defendant abjured his previous testimony.*

[Middle English *abjuren*, from Old French *abjurer*, from Latin *abiūrāre* : *ab-*, away + *iūrāre*, to swear.]

RELATED WORDS:
    noun—**ab′ju·ra′tion** (ăb′jə-rā′shən)
    noun—**ab·jur′er**

ab·ro·gate (ăb′rə-gāt′)

transitive verb

Past participle and past tense: **ab·ro·gat·ed**
Present participle: **ab·ro·gat·ing**
Third person singular present tense: **ab·ro·gates**

To abolish, do away with, or annul, especially by authority: "*In 1982, we were told that this amendment meant that our existing Aboriginal and treaty rights were now part of the supreme law of the land, and could not be abrogated or denied by any government*" (Matthew Coon Come, *Native Americas*).

[Latin *abrogāre, abrogāt-* : *ab-*, away + *rogāre*, to ask.]

RELATED WORD:
   noun — **ab′ro·ga′tion** (ăb′rə-gā′shən)

ab·ste·mi·ous (ăb-stē′mē-əs *or* əb-stē′mē-əs)

adjective

1. Eating and drinking in moderation: "*Mr. Brooke was an abstemious man, and to drink a second glass of sherry quickly at no great interval from the first was a surprise to his system*" (George Eliot, *Middlemarch*). **2.** Characterized by abstinence or moderation: *The hermit led an abstemious way of life.*

[From Latin *abstēmius* : *abs-, ab-*, away + **tēmum*, liquor, variant of *tēmētum.*]

RELATED WORDS:
   adverb — **ab·ste′mi·ous·ly**
   noun — **ab·ste′mi·ous·ness**

4

ac·u·men (ăk′yə-mən *or* ə-kyo͞o′mən)

noun

Quickness and keenness of judgment or insight: "'*No, no, my dear Watson! With all respect for your natural acumen, I do not think that you are quite a match for the worthy doctor*'" (Arthur Conan Doyle, *The Adventure of the Missing Three-Quarter*).

[Latin *acūmen*, from *acuere*, to sharpen, from *acus*, needle.]

✍ USAGE NOTE: The pronunciation (ə-kyo͞o′mən), with stress on the second syllable, is an older, traditional pronunciation reflecting the word's Latin origin. In recent years it has been supplanted as the most common pronunciation of the word by a variant with stress on the first syllable, (ăk′yə-mən). In our 1997 Usage Panel survey, 68 percent of the Panelists chose this as their pronunciation, while 29 percent preferred the pronunciation with stress on the second syllable. The remaining 3 percent said they use both pronunciations.

5

an·te·bel·lum (ăn′tē-bĕl′əm)

adjective

Belonging to the period before a war, especially the American Civil War: *While vacationing in Georgia, we took a tour of stately antebellum houses.*

[From Latin *ante bellum*, before the war : *ante*, before + *bellum*, war.]

aus·pi·cious (ô-spĭsh′əs)

adjective

1. Attended by favorable circumstances; propitious: *My boss was in a good mood, so I thought it was an auspicious time to ask for a raise.* **2.** Marked by success; prosperous: *The auspicious fundraiser allowed the charity to donate hundreds of toys to the orphanage.*

[From Latin *auspicium*, bird divination, from *auspex, auspic-*, one who foretold the future by watching the flights of birds.]

RELATED WORDS:
> *adverb* — **aus·pic′ious·ly**
> *noun* — **aus·pic′ious·ness**

be·lie (bē-lī′ *or* bĭ-lī′)

transitive verb
> Past participle and past tense: **be·lied**
> Present participle: **be·ly·ing**
> Third person singular present tense: **be·lies**

1. To give a false representation to; misrepresent: *"He spoke roughly in order to belie his air of gentility"* (James Joyce, *Dubliners*). **2.** To show to be false; contradict: *Their laughter belied their outward anger.*

[Middle English *bilien*, from Old English *belēogan*, to deceive with lies.]

RELATED WORD:
> *noun* — **be·li′er**

"He spoke roughly in order to **belie** his air of gentility, for his entry had been followed by a pause of talk. His face was heated. To appear natural he pushed his cap back on his head and planted his elbows on the table."

— James Joyce,
Dubliners

8

bel·li·cose (bĕl′ĭ-kōs′)

adjective

Warlike or <u>hostile</u> in manner or temperament: *The nations exchanged bellicose rhetoric over the border dispute.*

[Middle English, from Latin *bellicōsus,* from *bellicus,* of war, from *bellum,* war.]

RELATED WORDS:
> *adverb* — **bel′li·cose′ly**
> *noun* — **bel′li·cos′i·ty** (bĕl′ĭ-kŏs′ĭ-tē)
> *noun* — **bel′li·cose′ness**

9

bowd·ler·ize (bōd′lə-rīz′ *or* boud′lə-rīz′)

transitive verb
> Past participle and past tense: **bowd·ler·ized**
> Present participle: **bowd·ler·iz·ing**
> Third person singular present tense: **bowd·ler·iz·es**

To remove material that is considered objectionable or offensive from (a book, for example); expurgate: *The publisher bowdlerized the bawdy 18th-century play for family audiences.*

[After Thomas *Bowdler* (1754–1825), who published an expurgated edition of Shakespeare in 1818.]

RELATED WORDS:
> *noun* — **bowd′ler·ism**
> *noun* — **bowd′ler·i·za′tion**
>> (bōd′lər-ĭ-zā′shən)
>> *or* boud′lər-ĭ-zā′shən)
> *noun* — **bowd′ler·iz′er**

10

chi·can·er·y (shĭ-kā′nə-rē *or* chĭ-kā′nə-rē)

noun

Deception by trickery or sophistry: *"The successful man . . . who has risen by conscienceless swindling of his neighbors, by deceit and chicanery, by unscrupulous boldness and unscrupulous cunning, stands toward society as a dangerous wild beast"* (Theodore Roosevelt, *The Strenuous Life*).

[From *chicane*, to deceive, from French *chicaner*, from Old French, to quibble.]

11

chro·mo·some (krō′mə-sōm′)

noun

1. A threadlike linear strand of DNA and associated proteins in the nucleus of eukaryotic cells that carries the genes and functions in the transmission of hereditary information: *Chromosomes occur in pairs in all of the cells of eukaryotes except the reproductive cells.* **2.** A circular strand of DNA in bacteria that contains the hereditary information of the cell.

[*chromo-*, colored (from Greek *khrōma*, color) + *-some*, body (from Greek *sōma*).]

RELATED WORDS:
  adjective— **chro′mo·som′al** (krō′mə-sō′məl)
  adjective— **chro′mo·som′ic** (krō′mə-sō′mĭk)

12

churl·ish (chûr′lĭsh)

adjective

1. Of, like, or befitting a churl; boorish or vulgar. **2.** Having a bad disposition; <u>surly</u>: *"He is as valiant as the lion, churlish as the bear"* (William Shakespeare, *Troilus and Cressida*).

[From *churl*, rude person, from Middle English, from Old English *ceorl*, peasant.]

RELATED WORDS:
  adverb — **chur′lish·ly**
  noun — **chur′lish·ness**

13

cir·cum·lo·cu·tion (sûr′kəm-lō-kyōō′shən)

noun

1. The use of unnecessarily wordy and indirect language: *"There lives no man who at some period has not been tormented, for example, by an earnest desire to tantalize a listener by circumlocution"* (Edgar Allan Poe, *The Imp of the Perverse*). **2.** Evasiveness in speech or writing. **3.** A roundabout expression: *"At such time as"* is a circumlocution for the word *"when."*

[Middle English *circumlocucioun*, from Latin *circumlocūtiō*, *circumlocūtiōn-*, from *circumlocūtus*, past participle of *circumloquī* : *circum-*, around + *loquī*, to speak.]

RELATED WORD:
  adjective — **cir′cum·loc′u·to′ry**
      (sûr′kəm-lŏk′yə-tôr′ē)

"There lives no man who at some period
has not been tormented, for example, by
an earnest desire to tantalize a listener
by circumlocution."

— Edgar Allan Poe,
The Imp of the Perverse

14
cir·cum·nav·i·gate (sûr′kəm-năv′ĭ-gāt′)

transitive verb

Past participle and past tense: **cir·cum·nav·i·gat·ed**
Present participle: **cir·cum·nav·i·gat·ing**
Third person singular present tense: **cir·cum·nav·i·gates**

1. To proceed completely around: *"The whale he had struck must also have been on its travels; no doubt it had thrice circumnavigated the globe"* (Herman Melville, *Moby-Dick*). **2.** To go around; circumvent: *I circumnavigated the downtown traffic by taking side streets on the west side of town.*

[*circum-*, around (from Latin) + *navigate*, to sail (from Latin *nāvigāre, nāvigāt-* : *nāvis,* ship + *agere,* to drive, lead).]

RELATED WORDS:
noun — **cir′cum·nav·i·ga′tion**
(sûr′kəm-năv′ĭ-gā′shən)
noun — **cir′cum·nav′i·ga′tor**

15

de·cid·u·ous (dĭ-sĭj′ōo-əs)

adjective

1. Shedding or losing foliage at the end of the growing season: *"Orange-picking begins in December and overlaps the pruning of the deciduous orchards"* (Mary Austin, *Art Influence in the West*). **2.** Falling off or shed at a specific season or stage of growth: *Male deer have deciduous antlers.* **3.** Not lasting; ephemeral.

[From Latin *dēciduus*, from *dēcidere*, to fall off : *dē-*, down from + *cadere*, to fall.]

RELATED WORDS:
  adverb — **de·cid′u·ous·ly**
  noun — **de·cid′u·ous·ness**

16

del·e·te·ri·ous (dĕl′ĭ-tîr′ē-əs)

adjective

Having a harmful effect; injurious: *"I will follow that system of regimen which, according to my ability and judgment, I consider for the benefit of my patients, and abstain from whatever is deleterious and mischievous"* (Hippocratic Oath).

[From Greek *dēlētērios*, from *dēlētēr*, destroyer, from *dēleisthai*, to harm.]

RELATED WORDS:
  adverb — **del′e·te′ri·ous·ly**
  noun — **del′e·te′ri·ous·ness**

dif·fi·dent (dĭf'ĭ-dənt *or* dĭf'ĭ-dĕnt')

adjective

Lacking or marked by a lack of self-confidence; shy and timid: *"He was too diffident to do justice to himself; but when his natural shyness was overcome, his behaviour gave every indication of an open affectionate heart"* (Jane Austen, *Sense and Sensibility*).

[Middle English, from Latin *diffīdēns, diffīdent-*, present participle of *diffīdere*, to mistrust : *dis-*, not, do the opposite of + *fīdere*, to trust.]

RELATED WORD:
   adverb — **dif'fi·dent·ly**

en·er·vate (ĕn'ər-vāt')

transitive verb
   Past participle and past tense: **en·er·vat·ed**
   Present participle: **en·er·vat·ing**
   Third person singular present tense: **en·er·vates**

To weaken or destroy the strength or vitality of: *"What is the nature of the luxury which enervates and destroys nations?"* (Henry David Thoreau, *Walden*).

[Latin *ēnervāre, ēnervāt-* : *ē-, ex-*, out of, from + *nervus*, sinew.]

RELATED WORDS:
   noun — **en'er·va'tion** (ĕn'ər-vā'shən)
   adjective — **en'er·va'tive**
   noun — **en'er·va'tor**

☙ **USAGE NOTE:** Sometimes people mistakenly use *enervate* to mean "to invigorate" or "to excite" by assuming that this word is a close cousin of *energize*. In fact, *enervate* means essentially the opposite. *Enervate* comes from Latin *nervus*, "sinew," and thus means "to cause to become 'out of muscle,'" that is, "to weaken or deplete of strength." *Enervate* has no historical connection with *energize*.

19 en·fran·chise (ĕn-frăn′chīz′)

transitive verb
> Past participle and past tense: **en·fran·chised**
> Present participle: **en·fran·chis·ing**
> Third person singular present tense: **en·fran·chis·es**

1. To endow with the rights of citizenship, especially the right to vote: *Many people who were enfranchised were nonetheless unable to vote because of onerous poll taxes.* **2.** To free, as from slavery or bondage.

[Middle English *enfraunchisen*, from Old French *enfranchir, enfranchiss-*, to set free : *en-*, intensive prefix + *franchir*, to free (from *franc*, free).]

RELATED WORD:
> *noun* — **en·fran′chise′ment**

e·piph·a·ny (ĭ-pĭf′ə-nē)

noun
   Plural: **e·piph·a·nies**

1. Epiphany a. A Christian feast celebrating the manifestation of the divine nature of Jesus to the Gentiles as represented by the Magi. **b.** January 6, on which date this feast is traditionally observed. **2.** A revelatory manifestation of a divine being. **3.** A sudden manifestation of the essence or meaning of something; a revelation: *"I experienced an epiphany, a spiritual flash that would change the way I viewed myself"* (Frank Maier, *Newsweek*).

[Middle English *epiphanie*, from Old French, from Late Latin *epiphania*, from Greek *epiphaneia*, manifestation, from *epiphainesthai*, to appear : *epi-*, forth + *phainein*, *phan-*, to show.]

RELATED WORD:
   adjective — **ep′i·phan′ic** (ĕp′ə-făn′ĭk)

21

e·qui·nox (ē′kwə-nŏks′ *or* ĕk′wə-nŏks′)

noun
Plural: **e·qui·nox·es**

1. Either of the two times during a year when the sun crosses the celestial equator and when the length of day and night are approximately equal: *The vernal equinox occurs on March 20 or 21, and the autumnal equinox occurs on September 22 or 23.* **2.** Either of two points on the celestial sphere at which the ecliptic intersects the celestial equator.

[Middle English, from Old French *equinoxe*, from Medieval Latin *aequinoxium*, from Latin *aequinoctium* : *aequi-*, equal + *nox, noct-*, night.]

RELATED WORD:
  adjective— **e′qui·noc′tial** (ē′kwə-nŏk′shəl *or* ĕk′wə-nŏk′shəl)

22

eu·ro or **Eu·ro** (yŏŏr′ō)

noun
Plural: **eu·ros** or **Eu·ros**

The basic unit of currency among members of the European Monetary Union: *Italy and France are two countries that have adopted the euro.*

[After *Europe.*]

ev·a·nes·cent (ĕv′ə-nĕs′ənt)

adjective

Vanishing or likely to vanish like vapor: *"Most certainly I shall find this thought a horrible vision—a maddening, but evanescent dream"* (Mary Wollstonecraft Shelley, *The Last Man*).

[From Latin *ēvānēscere*, to vanish : *ē-*, *ex-*, away + *vānēscere*, to disappear (from *vānus*, empty).]

RELATED WORDS:
> *verb* — **ev′a·nesce′** (ĕv′ə-nĕs′)
> *adverb* — **ev′a·nes′cent·ly**

ex·pur·gate (ĕk′spər-gāt′)

transitive verb
> Past participle and past tense: **ex·pur·gat·ed**
> Present participle: **ex·pur·gat·ing**
> Third person singular present tense: **ex·pur·gates**

To remove erroneous, vulgar, obscene, or otherwise objectionable material from (a book, for example) before publication: *The R-rated movie was expurgated before it was shown on network television.*

[Latin *expūrgāre*, *expūrgāt-*, to purify : *ex-*, intensive prefix + *pūrgāre*, to cleanse (from *pūrus*, pure).]

RELATED WORDS:
> *noun* — **ex′pur·ga′tion** (ĕk′spər-gā′shən)
> *noun* — **ex′pur·ga′tor**

25

fa·ce·tious (fə-sēʹshəs)

adjective

Playfully jocular; humorous: *The employee's facetious remarks were not appreciated during the meeting.*

[French *facétieux*, from *facétie*, jest, from Latin *facētia*, from *facētus*, witty.]

RELATED WORDS:
> *adverb* — **fa·ceʹtious·ly**
> *noun* — **fa·ceʹtious·ness**

26

fat·u·ous (făchʹo͞o-əs)

adjective

Foolish or silly, especially in a smug or self-satisfied way: *"'Don't you like the poor lonely bachelor?' he yammered in a fatuous way"* (Sinclair Lewis, *Main Street*).

[From Latin *fatuus*.]

RELATED WORDS:
> *adverb* — **fatʹu·ous·ly**
> *noun* — **fatʹu·ous·ness**

feck·less (fĕk′lĭs)

adjective

1. Lacking purpose or vitality; feeble or ineffective: "*She glowered at the rows of feckless bodies that lay sprawled in the chairs*" (Willa Cather, *The Song of the Lark*). **2.** Careless and irresponsible: *The feckless student turned in yet another late paper.*

[Scots *feck*, effect + *-less*.]

RELATED WORDS:
> *adverb* — **feck′less·ly**
> *noun* — **feck′less·ness**

fi·du·ci·ar·y (fĭ-dōō′shē-ĕr′ē *or* fĭ-dōō′shə-rē *or* fī-dōō′shē-ĕr′ē *or* fī-dōō′shə-rē)

adjective

1a. Of or relating to a holding of something in trust for another. **b.** Of or being a trustee or trusteeship. **c.** Held in trust. **2.** Of or consisting of legal tender, especially paper currency, authorized by a government but not based on or convertible into gold or silver.

noun
> Plural: **fi·du·ci·ar·ies**

One, such as a company director, that has a special relation of trust, confidence, or responsibility in certain obligations to others.

[Latin *fīdūciārius*, from *fīdūcia*, trust, from *fīdere*, to trust.]

"She was going to have a few things before she died. She realized that there were a great many trains dashing east and west on the face of the continent that night, and that they all carried young people who meant to have things. But the difference was that *she was going to get them!* That was all. Let people try to stop her! She glowered at the rows of **feckless** bodies that lay sprawled in the chairs. Let them try it once!"

—Willa Cather,
The Song of the Lark

fil·i·bus·ter (fĭl′ə-bŭs′tər)

noun

1a. The use of obstructionist tactics, especially pro-longed speechmaking, for the purpose of delaying legislative action. **b.** An instance of the use of such tactics: *The senator's filibuster lasted over 24 hours.* **2.** An adventurer who engages in a private military action in a foreign country.

verb
> Past participle and past tense: **fil·i·bus·tered**
> Present participle: **fil·i·bus·ter·ing**
> Third person singular present tense: **fil·i·bus·ters**

intransitive: **1.** To use obstructionist tactics in a legislative body. **2.** To take part in a private military action in a foreign country.

transitive: To use a filibuster against (a legislative measure, for example).

[From Spanish *filibustero*, freebooter, from French *flibustier*, from Dutch *vrijbuiter*, pirate, freebooter, from *vrijbuit*, plunder : *vrij*, free + *buit*, booty (from Middle Dutch *būte*, of Middle Low German origin).]

RELATED WORD:
> *noun* — **fil′i·bus′ter·er**

30

gam·ete (găm′ēt′ *or* gə-mēt′)

noun

A reproductive cell having the haploid number of chromosomes, especially a mature sperm or egg capable of fusing with a gamete of the opposite sex to produce the fertilized egg.

[New Latin *gameta*, from Greek *gametē*, wife, and *gametēs*, husband, from *gamein*, to marry, from *gamos*, marriage.]

RELATED WORD:
  adjective—**ga·met′ic** (gə-mĕt′ĭk)

31

gauche (gōsh)

adjective

Lacking grace or social polish; awkward or tactless: *"A good man often appears gauche simply because he does not take advantage of the myriad mean little chances of making himself look stylish"* (Iris Murdoch, *The Black Prince*).

[French, awkward, lefthanded, from Old French, from *gauchir*, to turn aside, walk clumsily, of Germanic origin.]

RELATED WORDS:
  adverb—**gauche′ly**
  noun—**gauche′ness**

ger·ry·man·der (jĕr′ē-măn′dər *or* gĕr′ē-măn′dər)

transitive verb

Past participle and past tense: **ger·ry·man·dered**
Present participle: **ger·ry·man·der·ing**
Third person singular present tense: **ger·ry·man·ders**

To divide (a geographic area) into voting districts so as to give unfair advantage to one party in elections.

noun

1. The act, process, or an instance of gerrymandering.
2. A district or configuration of districts differing widely in size or population because of gerrymandering.

[After Elbridge *Gerry* + *(sala)mander* (from the shape of an election district created while Gerry was governor of Massachusetts).]

WORD HISTORY: *"An official statement of the returns of voters for senators give[s] twenty nine friends of peace, and eleven gerrymanders."* So reported the May 12, 1813, edition of the *Massachusetts Spy.* A gerrymander sounds like a strange political beast, which it is, considered from a historical perspective. This beast was named by combining the word *salamander,* "a small lizardlike amphibian," with the last name of Elbridge Gerry, a former governor of Massachusetts. Gerry was immortalized in this word because an election district created by members of his party in 1812 looked like a salamander. The word is first recorded in April 1812 in reference to the creature or its caricature, but it soon came to mean not only "the action of shaping a district to gain political advantage" but also "any representative elected from such a district by that method." Within the same year, *gerrymander* was also recorded as a verb.

---

he·gem·o·ny (hĭ-jĕm′ə′nē *or* hĕj′ə-mō′nē)

noun

Plural: **he·gem·o·nies**

The predominant influence of a state, region, or group, over others: *The hegemony of communism in Eastern Europe crumbled in the late 1980s.*

[Greek *hēgemoniā,* from *hēgemōn,* leader, from *hēgeisthai,* to lead.]

RELATED WORDS:
adjective — **heg′e·mon′ic** (hĕj′ə-mŏn′ĭk)
noun & adjective — **he·gem′o·nist** (hə-jĕm′ə-nĭst)

〄 **USAGE NOTE:** *Hegemony* may be stressed on either the first or second syllable. In a 1988 survey of the Usage Panel, 72 percent of the Panelists preferred the latter pronunciation.

he·mo·glob·in (hē′mə-glō′bĭn)

noun

The iron-containing pigment in red blood cells of vertebrates, consisting of about 6 percent heme and 94 percent globin. In vertebrates, hemoglobin carries oxygen from the lungs to the tissues of the body and carries carbon dioxide from the tissues to the lungs.

[Ultimately short for *hematinoglobulin* : *hematin,* a compound formed from hemoglobin (*hemato-,* blood, from Greek *haima,* blood + *-in,* chemical suffix) + *globulin,* a kind of protein (*globule,* from French, from Latin *globulus,* diminutive of *globus,* sphere + *-in,* chemical suffix).]

"There is no safety in unlimited technological **hubris**, none in simple-minded trust of the Kremlin, and none in a confident affection for expanding thermonuclear arsenals."

— McGeorge Bundy,
New York Times Magazine

ho·mo·ge·ne·ous (hō′mō-jē′nē-əs
  or hō′mō-jēn′yəs)

adjective

1. Uniform in structure or composition: *"Although the
Vietnamese in America were at first a homogenous group,
in the course of five separate waves of immigration they
have encompassed a diverse cross-section of Vietnamese
society"* (Lowell Weiss, *Atlantic Monthly*). **2.** Of the
same or similar nature or kind. **3.** *Mathematics* Consisting of terms of the same degree or elements of the
same dimension.

[From Medieval Latin *homogeneus,* from Greek *homogenēs* :
homo-, same + *genos*, kind.]

RELATED WORDS:
  adverb — **ho′mo·ge′ne·ous·ly**
  noun — **ho′mo·ge′ne·ous·ness**

hu·bris (hyōō′brĭs)

noun

Overbearing pride or presumption; arrogance: *"There is
no safety in unlimited technological hubris"* (McGeorge
Bundy, *New York Times Magazine*).

[Greek, excessive pride, wanton violence.]

RELATED WORDS:
  adjective — **hu·bris′tic** (hyōō-brĭs′tĭk)
  adverb — **hu·bris′tic·al·ly**

hy·pot·e·nuse (hī-pŏt′n-ōōs′)

noun

The side of a right triangle opposite the right angle: *"You cannot write a textbook of geometry without reference to a hypotenuse and triangles and a rectangular parallelepiped. You simply have to learn what those words mean or do without mathematics"* (Hendrick Van Loon, The Story of Mankind).

[Latin *hypotēnūsa,* from Greek *hupoteinousa,* from feminine present participle of *hupoteinein,* to stretch or extend under : *hupo-,* under + *teinein,* to stretch.]

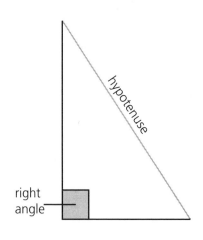

THE HYPOTENUSE
OF A RIGHT TRIANGLE

im·peach (ĭm-pēch′)

transitive verb
   Past participle and past tense: **im·peached**
   Present participle: **im·peach·ing**
   Third person singular present tense: **im·peach·es**

1a. To make an accusation against (a person). **b.** To charge (a public official) with improper conduct in office before a proper tribunal: *The House of Representatives impeached Andrew Johnson in 1868 and Bill Clinton in 1998; neither was convicted.* **2.** To challenge the validity of; try to discredit: *The lawyer impeached the witness's credibility with a string of damaging questions.*

[Middle English *empechen*, to impede, accuse, from Anglo-Norman *empecher*, from Late Latin *impedicāre*, to entangle : Latin *in-*, in + Latin *pedica*, fetter.]

RELATED WORDS:
   adjective—**im·peach′a·ble**
   noun—**im·peach′ment**

USAGE NOTE: When an irate citizen demands that a disfavored public official be impeached, the citizen clearly intends for the official to be removed from office. This popular use of *impeach* as a synonym of "throw out" (even if by due process) does not accord with the legal meaning of the word. As recent history has shown, when a public official is impeached, that is, formally accused of wrongdoing, this is only the start of what can be a lengthy process that may or may not lead to the official's removal from office. In strict usage, an official is impeached (accused), tried, and then convicted or acquitted. The vaguer use of *impeach* reflects disgruntled citizens' indifference to whether the official is forced from office by legal means or chooses to resign to avoid further disgrace.

39

in·cog·ni·to (ĭn′kŏg-nē′tō)

adjective & adverb

With one's identity disguised or concealed: *The spy traveled incognito into enemy territory.*

noun
   Plural: **in·cog·ni·tos**

The identity assumed by a person whose actual identity is disguised or concealed.

[Italian, from Latin *incognitus*, unknown : *in-*, not + *cognitus*, past participle of *cognōscere*, to learn, recognize.]

40

in·con·tro·vert·i·ble (ĭn-kŏn′trə-vûr′tə-bəl *or* ĭn′kŏn-trə-vûr′tə-bəl)

adjective

Impossible to dispute; unquestionable: *The lawyer presented incontrovertible proof of her client's innocence.*

[*in-*, not + *controvertible*, able to be opposed by argument, from *controvert*, to oppose by argument, back-formation from *controversy* (on the model of such pairs as *inverse, invert*), from Middle English *controversie*, from Latin *contrōversia*, from *contrōversus*, disputed: *contrō-*, variant of *contrā-*, against + *versus*, past participle of *vertere*, to turn.]

RELATED WORDS:
   noun—**in·con′tro·vert′i·bil′i·ty**
   adverb—**in·con′tro·vert′i·bly**

---

incognito / inculcate   **28**

41

in·cul·cate (ĭn-kŭl′kāt′ *or* ĭn′kŭl-kāt′)

transitive verb
    Past participle and past tense: **in·cul·ca·ted**
    Present participle: **in·cul·ca·ting**
    Third person singular present tense: **in·cul·cates**

1. To impress (something) upon the mind of another by frequent instruction or repetition; instill: "*In the jungle might is right, nor does it take long to inculcate this axiom in the mind of a jungle dweller, regardless of what his past training may have been*" (Edgar Rice Burroughs, *The Son of Tarzan*). **2.** To teach (others) by frequent instruction or repetition; indoctrinate: *inculcate the young with a sense of duty.*

[Latin *inculcāre, inculcāt-,* to force upon : *in-,* on + *calcāre,* to trample (from *calx, calc-,* heel).]

RELATED WORDS:
    noun — **in′cul·ca′tion** (ĭn′kŭl-kā′shən)
    noun — **in·cul′ca′tor**

in·fra·struc·ture (ĭn′frə-strŭk′chər)

noun

1. The basic facilities, services, and installations needed for the functioning of a community or society, such as transportation and communications systems, water and power lines, and public institutions including schools, post offices, and prisons: "*To be fair, none of us really knows how much the country's infrastructure—services to the desperate underclass—had improved during the ten years from when we left until the Revolution*" (Terence Ward, *Searching for Hassan*). **2.** The basic system or underlying structure of an organization.

[*infra-*, below (from Latin *īnfrā*) + *structure* (from Middle English, the process of building, from Latin *strūctūra*, from *strūctus*, past participle of *struere*, to construct).]

"Never in my life had I seen conditions as grim. To be fair, none of us really knows how much the country's **infrastructure** — services to the desperate underclass — had improved during the ten years from when we left until the Revolution. But one thing's certain. Whatever changes took place, it was too little, too late. Those forlorn dust heaps of villages, cut off from the world, with no medical facilities, no school, no decent roads to get goods to market. There seemed to be no hope at all."

— Terence Ward,
Searching for Hassan

in·ter·po·late (ĭn-tûr′pə-lāt′)

verb

    Past participle and past tense: **in·ter·po·la·ted**
    Present participle: **in·ter·po·la·ting**
    Third person singular present tense: **in·ter·po·lates**

transitive: **1.** To insert or introduce between other elements or parts. **2a.** To insert (material) into a text. **b.** To insert into a conversation. **3.** To change or falsify (a text) with new or incorrect material. **4.** *Mathematics* To estimate a value of (a function or series) between two known values: *The researchers had actual statistics for the years 1998, 2000, and 2002, and they interpolated the values for 1999 and 2001.*

intransitive: To make insertions or additions.

[Latin *interpolāre, interpolāt-*, to touch up, refurbish, from *interpolis*, refurbished; akin to *polīre*, to polish.]

RELATED WORDS:
    noun — **in·ter′po·la′tion** (ĭn-tûr′pə-lā′shən)
    adjective — **in·ter′po·la′tive**
    noun — **in·ter′po·la′tor**

i·ro·ny (ī′rə-nē *or* ī′ər-nē)

noun
    Plural: **i·ro·nies**

1a. The use of words to express something different from and often opposite to their literal meaning. **b.** An expression or utterance marked by a deliberate contrast between apparent and intended meaning. **c.** A literary

---

style employing such contrasts for humorous or rhetorical effect. **2a.** Incongruity between what might be expected and what actually occurs. **b.** An occurrence, result, or circumstance notable for such incongruity. **3.** The dramatic effect achieved by leading an audience to understand an incongruity between a situation and the accompanying speeches, while the characters in the play remain unaware of the incongruity; dramatic irony.

[French *ironie*, from Old French, from Latin *īrōnīa*, from Greek *eirōneia*, feigned ignorance, from *eirōn*, dissembler, probably from *eirein*, to say.]

RELATED WORDS:
> *adjective* — **i·ron′ic**
> *adverb* — **i·ron′i·cal·ly**

𝕗𝔞 **USAGE NOTE:** The words *ironic, irony,* and *ironically* are sometimes used of events and circumstances that might better be described as simply "coincidental" or "improbable," in that they suggest no particular lessons about human vanity or folly. The Usage Panel dislikes the looser use of these words; 78 percent reject the use of *ironically* in the sentence *In 1969 Susie moved from Ithaca to California where she met her husband-to-be, who, ironically, also came from upstate New York.* Some Panelists noted that this particular usage might be acceptable if Susie had in fact moved to California in order to find a husband, in which case the story could be taken as exemplifying the folly of supposing that we can know what fate has in store for us. By contrast, 73 percent accepted the sentence *Ironically, even as the government was fulminating against American policy, American jeans and videocassettes were the hottest items in the stalls of the market,* where the incongruity can be seen as an example of human inconsistency.

45
je·june (jə-jo͞on′)

adjective

1. Not interesting; dull: *"Let a professor of law or physic find his place in a lecture room, and there pour forth jejune words and useless empty phrases, and he will pour them forth to empty benches"* (Anthony Trollope, *Barchester Towers*). **2.** Lacking maturity; childish: *The coach was dismayed at the players' jejune behavior after they won the game.* **3.** Lacking in nutrition: *The sickly child suffered from a jejune diet.*

[From Latin *iēiūnus*, meager, dry, fasting.]

RELATED WORDS:
>   *adverb* — **je·june′ly**
>   *noun* — **je·june′ness**

46
ki·net·ic (kə-nĕt′ĭk *or* kī-nĕt′ĭk)

adjective

1. Of, relating to, or produced by motion: *Any object that is moving has kinetic energy.* **2.** Relating to or exhibiting kinesis (movement or activity of an organism in response to a stimulus such as light).

[Greek *kīnētikos*, from *kīnētos*, moving, from *kīnein*, to move.]

RELATED WORD:
>   *adverb* — **ki·net′i·cal·ly**

kow·tow (kou-tou′ *or* kou′tou′)

intransitive verb

Past participle and past tense: **kow·towed**
Present participle: **kow·tow·ing**
Third person singular present tense: **kow·tows**

1. To kneel and touch the forehead to the ground in expression of deep respect, worship, or submission, as formerly done in China. **2.** To show servile deference: *Because everyone on staff was afraid of being laid off, they all kowtowed to their strict boss.*

noun

1. The act of kneeling and touching the forehead to the ground: *"We were always greeted in a grassy area near the headmen's fortresses, where tents were pitched especially for me to receive kowtows, enjoy good food, and watch singing and dancing"* (Alai, *Red Poppies*). **2.** An obsequious act.

[From Chinese (Mandarin) *kòu tóu* : *kòu*, to knock + *tóu*, head.]

48

lais·sez faire also lais·ser faire
(lĕs′ā fâr′ *or* lā′zā fâr′)

noun

1. An economic doctrine that opposes governmental regulation of or interference in commerce beyond the minimum necessary for a free-enterprise system to operate according to its own economic laws. **2.** Noninterference in the affairs of others.

[French : *laissez*, second person plural imperative of *laisser*, to let, allow (from Latin *laxāre*, to loosen, from *laxus*, loose) + *faire*, to do (from Latin *facere*).]

49

lex·i·con (lĕk′sĭ-kŏn′)

noun
Plural: **lex·i·cons** or **lex·i·ca** (lĕk′sĭ-kə′)

1. A dictionary. **2.** A stock of terms used in a particular profession, subject, or style; a vocabulary: *The lexicon of anatomy includes terms such as "aorta" and "duodenum."*

[Medieval Latin, from Greek *lexikon (biblion)*, word (book), neuter of *lexikos*, of words, from *lexis*, word, from *legein*, to speak.]

RELATED WORDS:
> *adjective* — **lex′i·cal**
> *adverb* — **lex′i·cal·ly**

lo·qua·cious (lō-kwā′shəs)

adjective

Very talkative; garrulous: *The loquacious barber always told stories while cutting the customers' hair.*

[From Latin *loquāx, loquāc-,* from *loquī,* to speak.]

RELATED WORDS:
   adverb—**lo·qua′cious·ly**
   noun—**lo·qua′cious·ness**
   noun—**lo·quac′i·ty** (lō-kwăs′ĭ-tē)

lu·gu·bri·ous (lŏo-gōō′brē-əs)

adjective

Mournful, dismal, or gloomy, especially to an exaggerated or ludicrous degree: *"This croak was as lugubrious as a coffin"* (Stephen Crane, *The Sergeant's Private Madhouse*).

[From Latin *lūgubris,* from *lūgēre,* to mourn.]

RELATED WORDS:
   adverb—**lu·gu′bri·ous·ly**
   noun—**lu·gu′bri·ous·ness**

met·a·mor·pho·sis (mĕt′ə-môr′fə-sĭs)

noun

Plural: **met·a·mor·pho·ses** (mĕt′ə-môr′fə-sēz′)

1. A marked change in appearance, character, condition, or function; a transformation: "*I sought out the myths of metamorphosis, tales of the weaver Arachne, who hanged herself and was changed by Athena into a spider*" (Jennifer Ackerman, *Chance in the House of Fate*). **2.** *Biology* Change in the form and often habits of an animal during normal development after the embryonic stage. Metamorphosis includes, in insects, the transformation of a maggot into an adult fly and a caterpillar into a butterfly, and, in amphibians, the changing of a tadpole into a frog.

[Latin *metamorphōsis*, from Greek, from *metamorphoun*, to transform : *meta-*, meta- + *morphē*, form.]

RELATED WORDS:

adjective—**met′a·mor′phic** (mĕt′ə-môr′fĭk)
verb—**met′a·mor′phose** (mĕt′ə-môr′fōz′ *or* mĕt′ə-môr′fōs′)
adjective—**met′a·mor′phous** (mĕt′ə-môr′fəs)

53
mi·to·sis (mī-tō′sĭs)

noun
Plural: **mi·to·ses** (mī-tō′sēz)

The process in cell division by which the nucleus divides, typically consisting of four stages, prophase, metaphase, anaphase, and telophase, and normally resulting in two new nuclei, each of which contains a complete copy of the parental chromosomes. Division of the cytoplasm follows the division of the nucleus, resulting in the formation of two distinct cells.

[Greek *mitos*, warp thread + *-ōsis*, condition.]

RELATED WORDS:
adjective— **mi·tot′ic** (mī-tŏt′ĭk)
adverb— **mi·tot′i·cal·ly**

54
moi·e·ty (moi′ĭ-tē)

noun
Plural: **moi·e·ties**

1. A half: *"Tom divided the cake and Becky ate with good appetite, while Tom nibbled at his moiety"* (Mark Twain, *The Adventures of Tom Sawyer*). **2.** A part, portion, or share. **3.** Either of two kinship groups based on unilateral descent that together make up a tribe or society.

[Middle English *moite*, from Old French *meitiet, moitie*, from Late Latin *medietās*, from Latin, the middle, from *medius*, middle.]

nan·o·tech·nol·o·gy (năn′ə-těk-nŏl′ə-jē)

noun

The science and technology of building devices, such as electronic circuits, from individual atoms and molecules.

[*nano-*, at the molecular level (from Greek *nānos, nannos,* little old man, dwarf, from *nannās,* uncle) + *technology* (Greek *tekhnē,* art, skill + Greek *-logiā,* study, from *logos,* word).]

RELATED WORD:

noun— **nan′o·tech·nol′o·gist**

ni·hil·ism (nī′ə-lĭz′əm *or* nē′ə-lĭz′əm)

noun

1. *Philosophy* **a.** An extreme form of skepticism that denies that existence is real: *"Nihilism is not only despair and negation, but above all the desire to despair and to negate"* (Albert Camus, *The Rebel*). **b.** The belief that all values are baseless and that nothing can be known or communicated. **2.** The rejection of all distinctions in moral or religious value and a willingness to repudiate all previous theories of morality or religious belief. **3.** The belief that destruction of existing political or social institutions is necessary for future improvement. **4.** also **Nihilism** A movement of mid-19th-century Russia that scorned authority and believed in reason, material-ism, and radical change in society through terrorism and assassination. **5.** *Psychology* A delusion that the world or one's mind, body, or self does not exist.

[Latin *nihil*, nothing + *-ism.*]

RELATED WORDS:
noun — **ni′hi·list**
adjective — **ni′hi·lis′tic**
adverb — **ni′hi·lis′ti·cal·ly**

57

no·men·cla·ture (nō′mən-klā′chər
or nō-měn′klə-chər)

noun

1. A system of names used in an art or science: *The
nomenclature of mineralogy is a classification of types of
rock.* **2.** The procedure of assigning names to organisms listed in a taxonomic classification: *Our biology
teacher explained the rules of nomenclature for plants
and animals.*

[Latin *nōmenclātūra*, from *nōmenclātor*, nomenclator, a slave
who accompanied his master to tell him the names of people
he met, variant of *nōmenculātor* : *nōmen*, name + *calātor*,
servant, crier (from *calāre*, to call).]

58

non·sec·tar·i·an (nŏn′sĕk-târ′ē-ən)

adjective

Not limited to or associated with a particular religious
denomination: *The airport chapel conducts nonsectarian
services daily.*

[*non-*, not (from Middle English, from Old French, from
Latin *nōn*) + *sectarian*, partisan (*sect*, sect, ultimately from
Latin *sequī*, to follow + *-arian*, belonging to).]

RELATED WORD:
    noun—**non′sec·tar′i·an·ism**

no·ta·rize (nō′tə-rīz′)

transitive verb

Past participle and past tense: **no·ta·rized**
Present participle: **no·ta·riz·ing**
Third person singular present tense: **no·ta·riz·es**

To certify or attest to (the validity of a signature on a document, for example) as a notary public: *Before I submitted the sales agreement at the real estate office, it had to be notarized.*

[*notar(y)* (from Middle English *notarie*, from Old French, from Latin *notārius*, relating to shorthand, shorthand writer, from *nota*, mark) + *-ize.*]

RELATED WORD:
        noun — **no′ta·ri·za′tion** (nō′tə-rĭ-zā′shən)

ob·se·qui·ous
        (ŏb-sē′kwē-əs *or* əb-sē′kwē-əs)

adjective

Full of or exhibiting servile compliance; fawning: *The movie star was surrounded by a large group of obsequious assistants.*

[Middle English, from Latin *obsequiōsus*, from *obsequium*, compliance, from *obsequī*, to comply : *ob-*, to; + *sequī*, to follow.]

RELATED WORDS:
        adverb — **ob·se′qui·ous·ly**
        noun — **ob·se′qui·ous·ness**

"For they that are discontented under monarchy call it tyranny; and they that are displeased with aristocracy call it **oligarchy**: so also, they which find themselves grieved under a democracy call it anarchy."

—Thomas Hobbes,
Leviathan

61

ol·i·gar·chy (ŏl′ĭ-gär′kē *or* ō′lĭ-gär′kē)

noun
   Plural: **ol·i·gar·chies**

1a. Government by a few, especially by a small faction of persons or families: *"They that are displeased with aristocracy call it oligarchy"* (Thomas Hobbes, *Leviathan*). **b.** Those making up such a government. **2.** A state governed by a few persons.

[*olig(o)-*, few (from Greek *oligos*, little) + *-archy*, rule (from Greek *-arkhiā*, from *arkhein*, to rule).]

RELATED WORDS:
   adjective — **ol′i·gar′chic** (ŏl′ĭ-gär′kĭk
         or ō′lĭ-gär′kĭk)
   adjective — **ol′i·gar′chic·al**

om·nip·o·tent (ŏm-nĭp′ə-tənt)

adjective

Having unlimited or universal power, authority, or force; all-powerful: *"I began to instruct him in the knowledge of the true God . . . that He was omnipotent, and could do everything for us, give everything to us, take everything from us"* (Daniel Defoe, *Robinson Crusoe*).

noun

the Omnipotent God.

[Middle English, from Old French, from Latin *omnipotēns, omnipotent-* : *omni-*, all + *potēns*, present participle of *posse*, to be able.]

RELATED WORDS:
     noun — **om·nip′o·tence**
     noun — **om·nip′o·ten·cy**
     adverb — **om·nip′o·tent·ly**

63

or·thog·ra·phy (ôr-thŏg′rə-fē)

noun
   Plural: **or·thog·ra·phies**

1. The art or study of correct spelling according to established usage. **2.** The aspect of language study concerned with letters and their sequences in words. **3.** A method of representing a language or the sounds of language by written symbols; spelling: *The orthography of Spanish includes the letters* í *and* ñ.

[*ortho-*, straight, correct (from Greek *orthos*) + *-graphy*, writing (from Greek *-graphiā*, from *graphein*, to write).]

RELATED WORDS:
   noun — **or·thog′ra·pher**
   noun — **or·thog′ra·phist**
   adjective — **or′tho·graph′ic** (ôr′thə-grăf′ĭk)
   adverb — **or′tho·graph′i·cal·ly**

ox·i·dize (ŏk′sĭ-dīz′)

verb

   Past participle and past tense: **ox·i·dized**
   Present participle: **ox·i·diz·ing**
   Third person singular present tense: **ox·i·diz·es**

transitive **1.** To combine with oxygen; make into an oxide: *The metal fender had begun to oxidize, as evidenced by the large rust stains.* **2.** To increase the positive charge or valence of (an element) by removing electrons. **3.** To coat with oxide.

intransitive To become oxidized.

[*oxid(e)*, compound containing oxygen (from French : *ox(ygène)*, oxygen + *(ac)ide*, acid) + *-ize.*]

RELATED WORDS:
      adjective — **ox′i·di′za·ble**
      noun — **ox′i·di·za′tion** (ŏk′sĭ-dĭ-zā′shən)

pa·rab·o·la (pə-răb′ə-lə)

noun

A plane curve formed by the intersection of a right circular cone and a plane parallel to an element of the cone or by the locus of points equidistant from a fixed line and a fixed point not on the line.

[New Latin, from Greek *parabolē*, comparison, application, parabola (from the relationship between the line joining the vertices of a conic and the line through its focus and parallel to its directrix), from *paraballein*, to compare : *para-*, beside + *ballein*, to throw.]

RELATED WORD:
 adjective— **par′a·bol′ic** (păr′ə-bŏl′ĭk)

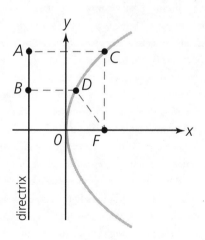

PARABOLA
Any point on a parabola is the same distance from the directrix
as it is from the focus. *AC = CF* and *BD = DF*.

---

par·a·digm (păr′ə-dīm′ *or* păr′ə-dĭm′)

noun

1. One that serves as pattern or model. **2.** A set or list of all the inflectional forms of a word or of one of its grammatical categories: *The Latin textbook outlined the paradigms of the different sets of regular verbs.* **3.** A set of assumptions, concepts, values, and practices that constitutes a way of viewing reality for the community that shares them, especially in an intellectual discipline.

[Middle English, example, from Late Latin *paradīgma*, from Greek *paradeigma*, from *paradeiknunai*, to compare : *para-*, alongside + *deiknunai*, to show.]

RELATED WORD:
adjective — **par′a·dig·mat′ic** (păr′ə-dĭg-măt′ĭk)

℞ **USAGE NOTE:** *Paradigm* first appeared in English in the 15th century, meaning "an example or pattern," and it still bears this meaning today: *Their company is a paradigm of small high-tech firms.* For nearly 400 years *paradigm* has also been applied to the patterns of inflections that are used to sort the verbs, nouns, and other parts of speech of a language into groups that are more easily studied. Since the 1960s, *paradigm* has been used in science to refer to a theoretical framework, as when Nobel Laureate David Baltimore cited colleagues' work that "*really established a new paradigm for our understanding of the causation of cancer.*" Thereafter, researchers in many different fields, including sociology and literary criticism, often saw themselves as working in or trying to break out of paradigms. Applications of the term in other contexts show that it can sometimes be used more loosely to mean "the prevailing view of things." In a 1994 Usage Panel survey, the Panelists split down the middle on these nonscientific uses of *paradigm.* Fifty-two percent disapproved of the sentence *The paradigm governing international competition and competitiveness has shifted dramatically in the last three decades.*

Paradigm of present tense Spanish verbs
with infinitives ending in -AR

-o	-amos
-as	-áis
-a	-an

hablar — to speak

First person singular:	*habl**o***
Second person singular:	*habl**as***
Third person singular:	*habl**a***
First person plural:	*habl**amos***
Second person plural:	*habl**áis***
Third person plural:	*habl**an***

pa·ram·e·ter (pə-răm′ĭ-tər)

noun

1. *Mathematics* **a.** A constant in an equation that varies in other equations of the same general form, especially such a constant in the equation of a curve or surface that can be varied to represent a family of curves or surfaces. **b.** One of a set of independent variables that express the coordinates of a point. **2a.** One of a set of measurable factors, such as temperature and pressure, that define a system and determine its behavior and are varied in an experiment. **b.** *(Usage Problem)* A factor that restricts what is possible or what results. **c.** A factor that determines a range of variations; a boundary: *The principal of the experimental school made sure that the parameters of its curriculum continued to expand.* **3.** *Statistics* A quantity, such as a mean, that is calculated from data and describes a population. **4.** *(Usage Problem)* A distinguishing characteristic or feature.

[New Latin *parametrum*, a line through the focus and parallel to the directrix of a conic : Greek *para-*, beside + Greek *metron*, measure.]

RELATED WORDS:
>   *verb*—**pa·ram′e·ter·ize′** (pə-răm′ə-tə-rīz′)
>   *adjective*—**par′a·met′ric** (păr′ə-mĕt′rĭk)
>   *adjective*—**par′a·met′ri·cal**
>   *adverb*—**par′a·met′ri·cal·ly**

𝒢 **USAGE NOTE:** The term *parameter,* which originates in mathematics, has a number of specific meanings in fields such as astronomy, electricity, crystallography, and statistics. Perhaps because of its ring of technical authority, it has been used more generally in recent years to refer to any factor that determines a range of variations and especially to a factor that restricts what

---

parameter   **52**

can result from a process or policy. In this use it often comes close to meaning "a limit or boundary." Some of these new uses have a clear connection to the technical senses of the word. For example, the provisions of a zoning ordinance that limit the height or density of new construction can be reasonably likened to mathematical parameters that establish the limits of other variables. Therefore one can say *The zoning commission announced new planning parameters for the historic district of the city.* But other uses go one step further and treat *parameter* as a high-toned synonym for *characteristic.* In the 1988 Usage Panel Survey, 80 percent of Panelists rejected this use of *parameter* in the example *The Judeo-Christian ethic is one of the important parameters of Western culture.*

Some of the difficulties with the nontechnical use of *parameter* appear to arise from its resemblance to the word *perimeter,* with which it shares the sense "limit," though the precise meanings of the two words differ. This confusion probably explains the use of *parameter* in a sentence such as *US forces report that the parameters of the mine area in the Gulf are fairly well established,* where the word *perimeter* would have expressed the intended sense more exactly. This example of a use of *parameter* was unacceptable to 61 percent of the Usage Panel.

"There had come an improvement in their **pecuniary** position, which earlier in their experience would have made them cheerful. Jude had quite unexpectedly found good employment at his old trade almost directly he arrived, the summer weather suiting his fragile constitution; and outwardly his days went on with that monotonous uniformity which is in itself so grateful after vicissitude."

— Thomas Hardy,
Jude the Obscure

pe·cu·ni·ar·y (pĭ-kyōō′nē-ĕr′ē)

adjective

1. Of or relating to money: *"There had come an improvement in their pecuniary position, which earlier in their experience would have made them cheerful"* (Thomas Hardy, *Jude the Obscure*). **2.** Requiring payment of money: *A speeding ticket is generally a pecuniary offense.*

[Latin *pecūniārius*, from *pecūnia*, property, wealth, money.]

RELATED WORD:
    adverb—**pe·cu′ni·ar′i·ly**

pho·to·syn·the·sis (fō′tō-sĭn′thĭ-sĭs)

noun

The process by which green plants and certain other organisms synthesize carbohydrates from carbon dioxide and water using light as an energy source. Most forms of photosynthesis release oxygen as a byproduct.

[*photo-*, light (from Greek *phōto-*, from *phōs, phōt-*) + *synthesis*, the building of chemical compounds (from Latin, collection, from Greek *sunthesis*, from *suntithenai*, to put together : *sun-*, with, together + *tithenai*, *the-*, to put).]

RELATED WORDS:
    verb—**pho′to·syn′the·size′**
      (fō′tō-sĭn′thĭ-sīz′)
    adjective—**pho′to·syn·thet′ic**
      (fō′tō-sĭn-thĕt′ĭk)
    adverb—**pho′to·syn·thet′i·cal·ly**

pla·gia·rize (plā′jə-rīz′)

verb

    Past participle and past tense: **pla·gia·rized**
    Present participle: **pla·gia·riz·ing**
    Third person singular present tense: **pla·gia·riz·es**

transitive **1.** To use and pass off (the ideas or writings of another) as one's own: *Gina plagiarized a science website by cutting and pasting large portions of its text into her paper.* **2.** To appropriate for use as one's own passages or ideas from (another): *Because Darren plagiarized Charles Dickens, the teacher could easily determine that he had cheated.*

intransitive To put forth as original to oneself the ideas or words of another: *Our teacher's policy is to fail any student who plagiarizes.*

[From Latin *plagiārius*, kidnapper, one who plagiarizes, from *plagium*, kidnapping, from *plaga*, net.]

RELATED WORD:
    noun— **pla′gia·riz′er**

plas·ma (plăz′mə) also **plasm** (plăz′əm)

noun

1. The clear yellowish fluid portion of blood or lymph in which cells are suspended. It differs from serum in that it contains fibrin and other soluble clotting elements. **2.** Blood plasma that has been sterilized and from which all cells have been removed, used in transfusions. **3.** The protoplasm or cytoplasm of a cell. **4.** The fluid portion of milk from which the curd has been separated by coagulation; whey. **5.** An electrically neutral state of matter similar to a gas but consisting of positively charged ions with most or all of their detached electrons moving freely about. Plasmas are produced by very high temperatures, as in the sun, and also by the ionization resulting from exposure to an electric current, as in a neon sign. Plasmas are distinct from solids, liquids, and normal gases.

[New Latin, from Late Latin, image, figure, from Greek, from *plassein*, to mold.]

RELATED WORDS:
adjective — **plas·mat′ic** (plăz-măt′ĭk)
adjective — **plas′mic** (plăz′mĭk)

pol·y·mer (pŏl′ə-mər)

noun

Any of numerous natural or synthetic compounds of usually high molecular weight consisting of repeated linked units, each a relatively light and simple molecule: *Some polymers, like cellulose, occur naturally, while others, like nylon, are artificial.*

[Greek *polumerēs*, consisting of many parts : *polu-*, many- + *meros*, part.]

pre·cip·i·tous (prĭ-sĭp′ĭ-təs)

adjective

1. Resembling a precipice; extremely steep. **2.** Having several precipices: *The hikers avoided the trail through the precipitous areas of the park.* **3.** *(Usage Problem)* Extremely rapid or abrupt; precipitate.

[Probably from obsolete *precipitious*, from Latin *praecipitium*, precipice, from *praeceps, praecipit-*, headlong : *prae-*, before, in front + *caput, capit-*, head.]

RELATED WORDS:
  adverb — **pre·cip′i·tous·ly**
  noun — **pre·cip′i·tous·ness**

🐌 **USAGE NOTE:** The adjective *precipitate* and the adverb *precipitately* were once applied to physical steepness but are now used primarily of rash, headlong actions: *Their precipitate entry into the foreign markets led to disaster. He withdrew precipitately from the race. Precipitous* currently means "steep" in both literal and figurative senses: *the precipitous rapids of the upper river; a precipitous drop in commodity prices.* But *precipitous* and *precipi-*

tously are also frequently used to mean "abrupt, hasty," which takes them into territory that would ordinarily belong to *precipitate* and *precipitately*: *their precipitous decision to leave.* This usage is a natural extension of the use of *precipitous* to describe a rise or fall in a quantity over time: *a precipitous increase in reports of measles* is also an abrupt or sudden event. Though this extended use of *precipitous* is well attested in the work of reputable writers, it is still widely regarded as an error.

74

qua·sar (kwā′sär′)

noun

An extremely distant, and thus old, celestial object whose power output is several thousand times that of the entire Milky Way galaxy. Some quasars are more than ten billion light years away from earth.

[*quas(i-stellar)* + *(st)ar.*]

quo·tid·i·an (kwō-tĭd′ē-ən)

adjective

Commonplace or ordinary, as from everyday experience: *"There's nothing quite like a real ... train conductor to add color to a quotidian commute"* (Anita Diamant, *Boston Magazine*).

[Middle English *cotidien*, from Old French, from Latin *quōtīdiānus*, from *quōtīdiē*, each day : *quot*, how many, as many as + *diē*, ablative of *diēs*, day.]

re·ca·pit·u·late (rē′kə-pĭch′ə-lāt′)

verb

Past participle and past tense: **re·ca·pit·u·lat·ed**
Present participle: **re·ca·pit·u·lat·ing**
Third person singular present tense: **re·ca·pit·u·lates**

transitive **1.** To repeat in concise form: *"Uninitiated readers can approach this bewitching new rogue's tale as if nothing had happened. Whatever took place previously is recapitulated, now bathed in the warm light of memory"* (Janet Maslin, *New York Times*). **2.** *Biology* To appear to repeat (the evolutionary stages of the species) during the embryonic development of the individual organism.

intransitive To make a summary: *At the end of my presentation about the solar system, the teacher asked me to recapitulate.*

[Latin *recapitulāre, recapitulāt-* : *re-*, again + *capitulum*, main point, heading, diminutive of *caput, capit-*, head.]

RELATED WORDS:
  noun — **re′ca·pit′u·la′tion**
           (rē′kə-pĭch′ə-lā′shən)
  adjective — **re′ca·pit′u·la′tive**
  adjective — **re′ca·pit′u·la·to′ry**

re·cip·ro·cal (rĭ-sĭp′rə-kəl)

adjective

1. Existing, done, or experienced on both sides: *The two chess players showed reciprocal respect throughout the match.* **2.** Done, given, felt, or owed in return: *After hearing the emcee's kind remark, the guest of honor felt obliged to make a reciprocal compliment.* **3.** Interchangeable; complementary: *The hardware store stocks reciprocal electric outlets.* **4.** *Grammar* Expressing mutual action or relationship. Used of some verbs and compound pronouns. **5.** *Mathematics* Of or relating to the reciprocal of a quantity. **6.** *Physiology* Of or relating to a neuromuscular phenomenon in which the inhibition of one group of muscles accompanies the excitation of another. **7.** *Genetics* Of or being a pair of crosses in which the male or female parent in one cross is of the same genotype or phenotype as the complementary female or male parent in the other cross.

noun

1. Something that is reciprocal to something else. **2.** *Mathematics* A number related to another in such a way that when multiplied together their product is 1. For example, the reciprocal of 7 is 1/7; the reciprocal of 2/3 is 3/2.

[From Latin *reciprocus*, alternating.]

RELATED WORDS:

    noun—**re·cip′ro·cal′i·ty**
    adverb—**re·cip′ro·cal·ly**
    noun—**rec′i·proc′i·ty** (rĕs′ə-prŏs′ĭ-tē)

rep·a·ra·tion (rĕp′ə-rā′shən)

noun

1. The act or process of making amends for a wrong. **2.** Something done or money paid to compensate or make amends for a wrong. **3. reparations** Compensation or remuneration required from a defeated nation as indemnity for damage or injury during a war. **4.** The act or process of repairing or the condition of being repaired.

[Middle English *reparacion*, from Old French, from Late Latin *reparātiō, reparātiōn-*, restoration, from Latin *reparātus*, past participle of *reparāre*, to repair : *re-*, again + *parāre*, to prepare.]

res·pi·ra·tion (rĕs′pə-rā′shən)

noun

1a. The act or process of inhaling and exhaling; breathing: *"Every sudden emotion, including astonishment, quickens the action of the heart, and with it the respiration"* (Charles Darwin, *The Expression of the Emotions in Man and Animal*). **b.** The act or process by which an organism without lungs, such as a fish or a plant, exchanges gases with its environment. **2a.** The oxidative process in living cells by which the chemical energy of organic molecules is released in metabolic steps involving the consumption of oxygen and the liberation of carbon dioxide and water. **b.** Any of various analogous metabolic processes by which certain organisms, such as fungi and anaerobic bacteria, obtain energy from organic molecules.

[Latin *respīrātiō, respīrātiōn-*, from *respīrātus*, past participle of *respīrāre*, to breathe again : *re-*, again + *spīrāre*, to breathe.]

RELATED WORDS:

    adjective — **re′spi·ra′tion·al**
    adverb — **re′spi·ra′tion·al·ly**
    verb — **re·spire′** (rĭ-spīr′)

"Every sudden emotion, including astonishment, quickens the action of the heart, and with it the **respiration.**"

— Charles Darwin,
*The Expression of the Emotions
in Man and Animal*

san·guine (săng′gwĭn)

adjective

1. Cheerfully confident; optimistic: *"Haggard and red-eyed, his hopes plainly had deserted him, his sanguine mood was gone, and all his worst misgivings had come back"* (Charles Dickens, *The Mystery of Edwin Drood*). **2a.** In medieval physiology, having blood as the dominant humor. **b.** Having the temperament and ruddy complexion once thought to be characteristic of this humor; passionate. **3a.** Of the color of blood; red: *"This fellow here, with envious carping tongue / Upbraided me about the rose I wear / Saying the sanguine colour of the leaves / Did represent my master's blushing cheeks"* (William Shakespeare, *Henry VI, Part I*). **b.** Of a healthy reddish color; ruddy: *Because he worked outdoors, the farmer had a sanguine complexion.*

[Middle English, from Old French *sanguin*, from Latin *sanguineus*, from *sanguis*, *sanguin-*, blood.]

RELATED WORDS:

> *adverb* — **san′guine·ly**
> *noun* — **san′guine·ness**
> *noun* — **san·guin′i·ty**

WORD HISTORY: The similarity in form between *sanguine*, "cheerfully optimistic," and *sanguinary*, "bloodthirsty," may prompt one to wonder how they have come to have such different meanings. The explanation lies in medieval physiology with its notion of the four humors or bodily fluids (blood, bile, phlegm, and black bile). The relative proportions of these fluids was thought to determine a person's temperament. If blood was the predominant humor, one had a ruddy face and a disposition marked by courage, hope, and a readiness to fall in love. Such a temperament was called *sanguine,* the Middle English ancestor of our word *sanguine.* The source of the Middle English word was Old French *sanguin,* itself from Latin *sanguineus.* Both the Old French and Latin words meant "bloody," "blood-colored," Old French *sanguin* having the sense "sanguine in temperament" as well. Latin *sanguineus* was in turn derived from *sanguis,* "blood," just as English *sanguinary* is. The English adjective *sanguine,* first recorded in Middle English before 1350, continues to refer to the cheerfulness and optimism that accompanied a sanguine temperament but no longer has any direct reference to medieval physiology.

so·lil·o·quy (sə-lĭl′ə-kwē)

noun
Plural: **so·lil·o·quies**

1. A dramatic or literary form of discourse in which a character talks to himself or herself or reveals his or her thoughts when alone or unaware of the presence of other characters: *Shakespeare employs soliloquy in most of his plays.* **2.** A specific speech or piece of writing in this form of discourse: *"To be or not to be" is the beginning of a famous soliloquy in* Hamlet.

[Late Latin *sōliloquium* : Latin *sōlus*, alone + Latin *loquī*, to speak.]

RELATED WORDS:

> *noun* — **so·lil′o·quist** (sə-lĭl′ə-kwĭst)
> *verb* — **so·lil′o·quize** (sə-lĭl′ə-kwīz′)
> *noun* — **so·lil′o·quiz′er** (sə-lĭl′ə-kwī′zər)

sub·ju·gate (sŭb′jə-gāt′)

transitive verb
> Past participle and past tense: **sub·ju·gat·ed**
> Present participle: **sub·ju·gat·ing**
> Third person singular present tense: **sub·ju·gates**

1. To bring under control; conquer: *The intention of the conquistadors was to subjugate the peoples of the New World.* **2.** To make subservient or submissive; subdue: *The new owners subjugated the defiant workers by threatening layoffs.*

[Middle English *subjugaten,* from Latin *subiugāre, subiugāt-* : *sub-,* under + *iugum,* yoke.]

RELATED WORDS:
> *noun*—**sub′ju·ga′tion** (sŭb′jə-gā′shən)
> *noun*—**sub′ju·ga′tor** (sŭb′jə-gā′tər)

suf·fra·gist (sŭf′rə-jĭst)

noun

An advocate of the extension of political voting rights, especially to women: *Tireless suffragists worked to ensure the passage of the Nineteenth Amendment in 1920.*

[*suffrag(e)* (ultimately from Latin *suffrāgium,* the right to vote, from *suffrāgārī,* to express support : *sub-,* under, in support of + *frāgārī,* to vote) + *-ist.*]

RELATED WORD:
> *noun*—**suf′fra·gism** (sŭf′rə-jĭz′əm)

su·per·cil·i·ous (soo′pər-sĭl′ē-əs)

adjective

Feeling or showing haughty disdain: *"Assuming his most supercilious air of distant superiority, he planted himself, immovable as a noble statue, upon the hearth, as if a stranger to the whole set"* (Fanny Burney, *Dr. Johnson and Fanny Burney*).

[Latin *superciliōsus,* from *supercilium,* eyebrow, pride : *super,* above + *cilium,* lower eyelid.]

RELATED WORDS:
> *adverb* — su′per·cil′i·ous·ly
> *noun* — su′per·cil′i·ous·ness

tau·tol·o·gy (tô-tŏl′ə-jē)

noun
> Plural: **tau·tol·o·gies**

1a. Needless repetition of the same sense in different words; redundancy. **b.** An instance of such repetition. **2.** *Logic* An empty or vacuous statement composed of simpler statements in a fashion that makes it logically true whether the simpler statements are factually true or false; for example, *Either it will rain tomorrow or it will not rain tomorrow.*

[Late Latin *tautologia,* from Greek *tautologiā,* from *tautologos,* redundant : *tauto-,* the same + *legein,* to say.]

RELATED WORDS:
> *adjective* — tau′to·log′i·cal (tôt′l-ŏj′ĭ-kəl)
> *adverb* — tau′to·log′i·cal·ly

tax·on·o·my (tăk-sŏn′ə-mē)

noun
> Plural: **tax·on·o·mies**

1. The classification of organisms in an ordered system that indicates natural relationships. **2.** The science, laws, or principles of classification; systematics. **3.** Division into ordered groups or categories.

[French *taxonomie* : Greek *taxis*, arrangement + *-nomie*, method (from Greek *-nomiā*, from *nomos*, law).]

RELATED WORDS:
> *adjective* — **tax′o·nom′ic** (tăk′sə-nŏm′ĭk)
> *adverb* — **tax′o·nom′i·cal·ly**
> *noun* — **tax·on′o·mist** (tăk-sŏn′ə-mĭst)

tec·ton·ic (tĕk-tŏn′ĭk)

adjective

1. Of or relating to the forces involved in forming the geological features, such as mountains, continents, and oceans, of the earth's lithosphere. The processes of plate tectonics, such as mountain building, are tectonic events. **2a.** Relating to construction or building. **2b.** Architectural.

[Late Latin *tectonicus*, from Greek *tektonikos*, from *tektōn*, builder.]

RELATED WORD:
> *adverb* — **tec·ton′i·cal·ly**

88

tem·pes·tu·ous (tĕm-pĕs′chōō-əs)

adjective

1. Of, relating to, or resembling a tempest: *"The 31st of January was a wild, tempestuous day: there was a strong north wind, with a continual storm of snow drifting on the ground and whirling through the air"* (Anne Brontë, *Agnes Grey*). **2.** Characterized by violent emotions or actions; tumultuous; stormy: *"For perhaps the first time in her life she thought of him as a man, young, unhappy, tempestuous, full of desires and faults"* (Virginia Woolf, *Night and Day*).

[Middle English, from Late Latin *tempestuōsus*, from *tempestūs*, tempest, variant of *tempestās*.]

RELATED WORDS:
    adverb — **tem·pes′tu·ous·ly**
    noun — **tem·pes′tu·ous·ness**

89

ther·mo·dy·nam·ics (thûr′mō-dī-năm′ĭks)

noun

1. *(used with a singular verb)* The branch of physics that deals with the relationships and conversions between heat and other forms of energy. **2.** *(used with a plural verb)* Thermodynamic phenomena and processes.

[*thermo-*, heat (from Greek *thermē*, heat, from *thermos*, warm) + *dynamics*, study of motion (from Greek *dunamikos*, powerful, from *dunamis*, power, from *dunasthai*, to be able).]

RELATED WORD:
    adjective — **ther′mo·dy·nam′ic**

"She wondered what he was looking for; were there waves beating upon a shore for him, too, she wondered, and heroes riding through the leaf-hung forests? For perhaps the first time in her life she thought of him as a man, young, unhappy, **tempestuous**, full of desires and faults."

— Virginia Woolf,
Night and Day

to·tal·i·tar·i·an (tō-tăl′ĭ-târ′ē-ən)

adjective

Of, relating to, being, or imposing a form of government in which the political authority exercises absolute and centralized control over all aspects of life, the individual is subordinated to the state, and opposing political and cultural expression is suppressed: "*A totalitarian regime crushes all autonomous institutions in its drive to seize the human soul*" (Arthur M. Schlesinger, Jr., *Cycles of American History*).

noun

A practitioner or supporter of such a government.

[*total* + *(author)itarian*]

RELATED WORD:
   noun — **to·tal′i·tar′i·an·ism**
        (tō-tăl′ĭ-târ′ē-ə-nĭz′əm)

unc·tu·ous (ŭngk′chōō-əs)

adjective

1. Characterized by affected, exaggerated, or insincere earnestness: *I didn't believe a word that the unctuous spokesperson said.* **2.** Having the quality or characteristics of oil or ointment; slippery: "*They had march'd seven or eight miles already through the slipping unctuous mud*" (Walt Whitman, *Specimen Days*). **3.** Containing or composed of oil or fat.

[Middle English, from Old French *unctueus*, from Medieval Latin *ūnctuōsus*, from Latin *ūnctum*, ointment, from neuter past participle of *unguere*, to anoint.]

RELATED WORDS:

> *noun*—**unc′tu·os′i·ty** (ŭngk′chōō-ŏs′ĭ-tē)
> *adverb*—**unc′tu·ous·ly**
> *noun*—**unc′tu·ous·ness**

92

u·surp (yōō-sûrp′ *or* yōō-zûrp′)

verb

> Past participle and past tense: **u·surped**
> Present participle: **u·surp·ing**
> Third person singular present tense: **u·surps**

transitive **1.** To seize and hold (the power or rights of another, for example) by force and without legal authority: *"The principle that one class may usurp the power to legislate for another is unjust"* (Susan B. Anthony, quoted in Ida Husted Harper's *The Life and Work of Susan B. Anthony*). **2.** To take over or occupy without right: *The squatters illegally usurped the farmer's land.*

intransitive To seize another's place, authority, or possession wrongfully.

[Middle English *usurpen*, from Old French *usurper*, from Latin *ūsūrpāre*, to take into use, usurp.]

RELATED WORDS:

> *noun*—**u′sur·pa′tion** (yōō′sər-pā′shən
>   *or* yōō′zər-pā′shən)
> *noun*—**u·surp′er**

vac·u·ous (văk′yōō-əs)

adjective

1a. Lacking intelligence; stupid. **b.** Devoid of substance or meaning; inane: *The interview with the celebrity produced a series of vacuous comments.* **c.** Devoid of expression; vacant: *"The narrow, swinelike eyes were open, no more vacuous in death than they had been in life"* (Nicholas Proffitt, *The Embassy House*). **2.** Devoid of matter; empty.

[From Latin *vacuus*, empty.]

RELATED WORDS:
  adverb — **vac′u·ous·ly**
  noun — **vac′u·ous·ness**

ve·he·ment (vē′ə-mənt)

adjective

Forceful or intense in expression, emotion, or conviction; fervid: *The senator issued a vehement denial regarding the report linking him to a scandal.*

[Middle English, from Old French, from Latin *vehemēns, vehement-*, perhaps from *vehere*, to carry.]

RELATED WORDS:
  noun — **ve′he·mence**
  noun — **ve′he·men·cy**
  adverb — **ve′he·ment·ly**

vor·tex (vôr′tĕks′)

noun

Plural: **vor·tex·es** *or* **vor·ti·ces** (vôr′tĭ-sēz′)

1. A spiral motion of fluid, especially a whirling mass of water or air that sucks everything near it toward its center. Eddies and whirlpools are examples of vortexes. **2.** A place or situation regarded as drawing into its center all that surrounds it: *"Madam, is it not better that he showed repentance than that he never showed it at all? Better to atone for one minute than live in a vortex of despair?"* (Edna O'Brien, *In The Forest*).

[Latin *vortex, vortic-*, variant of *vertex*, from *vertere*, to turn.]

win·now (wĭn′ō)

verb

> Past participle and past tense: **win·nowed**
> Present participle: **win·now·ing**
> Third person singular present tense: **win·nows**

transitive **1.** To separate the chaff from (grain) by means of a current of air. **2.** To blow (chaff) off or away. **3.** To examine closely in order to separate the good from the bad; sift: *The judges winnowed a thousand essays down to six finalists.* **4a.** To separate or get rid of (an undesirable part); eliminate: *The accountant was adept at winnowing out errors in the spreadsheet.* **b.** To sort or select (a desirable part); extract: *The investigators winnowed the facts from the testimony.* **5.** To blow on; fan: *A breeze winnowed the grass.*

intransitive **1.** To separate grain from chaff. **2.** To separate the good from the bad.

noun

1. A device for winnowing grain. **2.** An act of winnowing.

[Middle English *winnewen*, alteration of *windwen*, from Old English *windwian*, from *wind*, wind.]

RELATED WORD:

> *noun* — **win′now·er**

"Such is thy pow'r, nor are thine orders vain,

O thou the leader of the mental train:

In full perfection all thy works are **wrought**

And thine the sceptre o'er the realms of thought."

— Phillis Wheatley,
"On Imagination"

wrought (rôt)

verb

A past tense and a past participle of **work**: *"In full perfection all thy works are wrought/And thine the sceptre o'er the realms of thought"* (Phillis Wheatley, "On Imagination").

adjective

1. Put together; created: *The jewel thieves concocted a carefully wrought plan.* **2.** Shaped by hammering with tools. Used chiefly of metals or metalwork: *The horseshoe was made of wrought iron.*

[Middle English *wroght*, from Old English *geworht*, past participle of *wyrcan*, to work.]

xen·o·phobe (zĕn′ə-fōb′ *or* zē′nə-fōb′)

noun

A person unduly fearful or contemptuous of that which is foreign, especially of strangers or foreign peoples.

[*xeno-*, a stranger (from Greek *xenos*) + *-phobe*, one who fears (from French, from Latin *-phobus*, from Greek *-phobos*, fearing, from *phobos*, fear).]

RELATED WORDS:
> *noun*—**xen′o·pho′bi·a** (zĕn′ə-fō′bē-ə
> *or* zē′nə-fō′bē-ə)
> *adjective*—**xen′o·pho′bic** (zĕn′ə-fō′bĭk
> *or* zē′nə-fō′bĭk)

99
yeo·man (yō′mən)

noun

Plural: **yeo·men**

1a. An attendant, servant, or lesser official in a royal or noble household. **b.** A yeoman of the guard. **2.** A petty officer performing chiefly clerical duties in the US Navy. **3.** An assistant or other subordinate, as of a sheriff. **4.** A diligent, dependable worker. **5.** A farmer who cultivates his own land, especially a member of a former class of small freeholders in England.

[Middle English *yoman*, perhaps from Old English **gēaman*, from Old Frisian *gāman*, villager : *gā*, region, district + *man*, man.]

RELATED WORD:
  noun — **yeo′man·ry**

100
zig·gu·rat (zĭg′ə-răt′)

noun

A temple tower of the ancient Assyrians and Babylonians, having the form of a terraced pyramid with successively receding stories.

[Akkadian *ziqqurratu*, temple tower, from *zaqāru*, to build high.]

Exercises to Further Improve and Enrich Your Vocabulary

Knowing and being able to use the *100 Words Every High School Graduate Should Know* is just one step that you can take to actively expand your vocabulary. Along with a good dictionary, such as *The American Heritage College Dictionary* or *The American Heritage High School Dictionary*, you can use these 100 words as a starting point to discover new words. The exercises shown below are among the many ways you can become more familiar with your dictionary and improve your vocabulary.

Building your vocabulary is an ongoing process that you can continue throughout your life. If you feel discouraged because you can't retain the definitions of all the words that you encounter, approach the task of expanding your vocabulary more slowly. If learning ten words a week is too difficult, aim for three, or five.

What is important is not the quantity of words you're learning. Rather, what is important is your process behind learning the words and the commitment you make to yourself to strengthen your vocabulary over time.

Choose ten words from the list of *100 Words Every High School Graduate Should Know*. Look these ten words up in your dictionary.

On each page that these ten words are listed, choose a new word whose meaning you do not know. Create a document on your computer and type in that word along with its definition, or write the word down on paper with its definition.

For example, the word **auspicious** appears on page 95 of the fourth edition of *The American Heritage College Dictionary* and *The American Heritage High School Dictionary*. Other words on that page that you might choose to learn include **austerity, australopithecine, Austronesia,** or **authenticate**.

Keep a record of the new words that you learn. Every so often, go back and refresh your memory by rereading the definitions to these words. Create sentences that use these words so that you can become comfortable using them.

EXERCISE II

Choose a magazine or newspaper that you like to read at least once a week. Create a document on your computer or start a journal in a notebook. Every time you read a word whose meaning you're unsure of, add that word to your computer file or journal.

Look up the word in your dictionary, and write or type out the definition. Does knowing the precise definition of the word help you better understand the article?

After you have acquired a list of ten words, memorize them until they are part of your active vocabulary.

EXERCISE III

Many of the words in the list of *100 Words Every High School Graduate Should Know* include terms from specific areas of study. For example, **parabola** and **hypotenuse** are both from the field of geometry. **Hemoglobin** and **photosynthesis** are from biology.

What fields of learning interest you? Create a list of ten words that you think people should know if they were to learn more about that topic. Think about how you would define those words, and compare your definitions with the definitions you find in your dictionary.